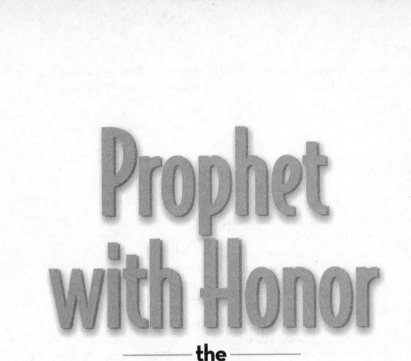

Prophet with Honor

---
the
Billy Graham
Story

William Martin

ZONDERkidz

ZONDERVAN.com/
AUTHORTRACKER
follow your favorite authors

We want to hear from you. Please send your comments about this book to us in care of zreview@zondervan.com. Thank you.

ZONDERKIDZ

Prophet with Honor: The Billy Graham Story
Copyright © 2013 by William Martin

This title is also available as a Zondervan ebook.
Visit www.zondervan.com/ebooks.

Requests for information should be addressed to:
Zonderkidz, 5300 Patterson Ave. SE, Grand Rapids, Michigan 49530

Library of Congress Cataloging-in-Publication Data

Martin, William C. (William Curtis), 1937-
    Prophet with honor : the Billy Graham story / William Martin. — Kids' abridged ed.
        p. cm.
    ISBN 978-0-310-71935-9 (softcover)
    1. Graham, Billy, 1918- –Juvenile literature. 2. Evangelists—United States—Biography—Juvenile literature. I. Title.
BV3785.G69   M278 2010
269'.2092—dc22
[B]

                                                                          2009054208

Cover design: Kris Nelson
Cover photo: Russ Busby
Interior design: Beth Shagene, Carlos Eluterio Estrada, & Greg Johnson/Textbook Perfect

Printed in the United States of America

13 14 15 16 17 18 19 20 /DCI/ 22 21 20 19 18 17 16 15 14 13 12 11 10 9 8 7 6 5 4 3 2 1

Contents

Prologue: Billy Graham, Evangelist 7

1. Billy Frank 11

2. College Boy 20

3. The Boy Preacher 26

4. Ruth 31

5. Youth for Christ 38

6. The Canvas Cathedral 46

7. The Hour of Decision 53

8. London and New York 63

9. They Are Precious in His Sight 71

10. Little Piney Cove 81

11. To All Nations 89

12. The Power and the Glory 96

13. Erasing Dividing Lines 106

14. Behind the Iron Curtain 110

15. Return to China 118

16. What Manner of Man? 123

17. The Last Days 137

Billy Graham, Evangelist

Billy Graham was ready.

On opening night, his white hair flowing down to his collar, the beloved old evangelist accepted a tremendous standing ovation, then signaled the audience to settle down. He had never shed tears easily, in part because of a problem with his tear ducts, but this time he could not stop them. "I have stars in my eyes," he said. "I can't see you very well just yet."

It was easy to see why he would be moved. Spread out before him like sheep on a thousand hills, the huge crowd—the total audience for the three nights was more than 230,000—may have been the most racially and culturally diverse crowd ever to attend a Billy Graham Crusade. It was about as diverse an audience as ever gathered anywhere for any reason.

Billy spoke, and his voice was clear and strong. He stood each night throughout all three sermons, using the stool only at the end. The sermons were short—about fifteen minutes—but the response was great. Nearly 10,000 people streamed forward when he gave the familiar invitation: "I'm going to ask you to come. Come now."

And the giant choir led the multitude in the encouraging hymn "Just As I Am."

It was fitting that the final revival in Billy Graham's long career would be held in New York City, the scene of his great 1957 "crusade" (the name he used for his revivals), when he filled Madison Square Garden every night from late May until early September. He had wanted to return to the Garden, but he knew the crowds would be too large. Instead, he and his advisers chose Corona Park, the site of the 1964–65 New York World's Fair.

Billy was eighty-six years old and in bad health. His sight and hearing were failing. Two serious falls had put him in the hospital for long periods in 2004. Reporters who interviewed him in the weeks before the June 2005 event said that he seemed feeble. The powerful voice that had helped make him famous was sometimes so weak they could barely hear it. At times he seemed to grope for words as he tried to answer simple questions. They wondered how he could possibly preach to a large crowd.

But at a press conference two days before the crusade was to begin, Billy had improved. His voice was stronger and he answered questions without hesitation. Newspapers continued to report that he would be able to sit on a high stool behind the large pulpit and that his son Franklin would take over if his father couldn't finish a sermon. They need not have worried. He remained off-stage in an air-conditioned tent until minutes before he was to preach. Then he slowly walked to the platform, using a walker and supported by Franklin at his side.

During his long career as an evangelist, Billy Graham preached the gospel of Christ to nearly 215 million people at gatherings in more than 185 countries, and over television to hundreds of millions more. At least 3.2 million people are known to have made "Decisions for Christ" as a result of his preaching. The actual number is unknown, but undoubtedly far, far larger.

No other evangelist in the history of Christianity has come close to reaching so many people. For more than half a century, Billy Graham was among the most famous and admired men in the world, but his fame never caused him to waver from his commitment to Christ and his lifelong determination to "do some great thing for God."

This book tells the story of the life and ministry of this remarkable man.

Billy Frank

Thanksgiving was still a week away, but as the late-autumn light started to fade on that cold, crystal-clear November 7 in 1918, Frank and Morrow Graham were already thanking God for the wonderful gift of their newborn son. They did not imagine that this tiny creature, wiggling his toes as his father examined him proudly by the light of the evening fire, would one day become the most famous preacher in the world.

The Grahams were devout Christians. They prayed on the first day of his life that Billy Frank—his proper name was William Franklin Graham Jr.—would one day feel that God wanted him to do something special.

Morrow Graham was small. Her clear blue eyes and long blonde hair gave her a delicate look. But her strong chin and bright smile caused people to think of her as having a strong will, which was true, and good character, also true.

Frank Graham was large and strong, with dark wavy hair and steel-blue eyes. He enjoyed telling jokes and stories, but no one thought of him as fun loving. He worked so hard on the family's dairy farm outside Charlotte, North Carolina, that he found it difficult to relax or to play. Billy Frank and his brother, Melvin, and his sisters, Catherine and Jean, couldn't remember their father ever playing a game or going fishing. On the few times when he took them to the seashore, he would roll up his trousers, splash around in the shallow water for a few minutes in his bare feet, then sit off to one side until it was time to go home. Because he was such a hard worker, he built the dairy farm into one of the largest in the area. He built his family a handsome two-story brick home that had indoor plumbing and electricity—rare for a country home in those days.

Billy Frank sometimes tested his mother's patience and nerves. He was described as "running and zooming" through the house. He turned over baskets full of eggs and knocked plates from the kitchen table. Once he shoved a bureau chest down a flight of stairs just to see what would happen.

"There was never any quietness about Billy," his mother said. "He was always tumbling over something. He was a handful. I was relieved when he started school."

At one point the Grahams took him to a doctor, complaining that "He never wears down." Today he would probably be called "hyperactive," but that word hadn't

Billy on extreme left, in black robe, graduating from Sunday school primary department at age six.

been invented yet. The doctor said, "It's just the way he's built."

Despite his antics, Billy Frank was a sweet-natured child. People liked him. The first words he ever put into a complete sentence were "Here comes Daddy, Sugar Baby." It was something he had heard his mother say.

His mother taught him the value of being thoughtful toward others. On the second day of first grade, his mother suggested he take a small bouquet of flowers to his teacher. He did, even though he had been embarrassed. The teacher was quite pleased, which also pleased him. From then on until he was fifteen or sixteen, he seldom let a week go by without going into the woods behind their big barn to gather a handful of wildflowers or to find some other treasure to bring home to his mother.

The Graham home was not all sugar babies and wildflowers. Frank and Morrow Graham were stern parents. They held their children to strict standards, enforced by frequent spankings. Billy Frank felt the sting of his mother's hickory switches and the bite of his father's belt hundreds of times during his first dozen years. Looking back, his mother admitted that she thought they could have gotten by with a lighter touch. "I think I would use a lot more psychology today."

From the beginning, Frank and Morrow Graham dedicated their marriage to God. On their wedding night, they read the Bible and prayed together. Each night in their home they had devotions. They attended a small, strict Presbyterian church and taught their children the Bible from an early age. Morrow drummed Bible verses into Billy Frank's head as she scrubbed his back in the washtub. The first one she taught him was one of the most famous passages in the Bible, John 3:16: "For God so loved the world, that he gave his only begotten son, that whosoever believeth in him should not perish, but have everlasting life."

Billy Frank's mother kept a Scripture calendar on the wall of the breakfast room. Each morning she tore off a verse the children were expected to memorize before they left for school. During the summer, they had to learn the verse before they went out to play. They prayed before every meal. Each evening after dinner, they would gather in the family room for devotions. Their mother would read Scripture and other inspirational material, and their father would pray. The children, as soon as they were old enough, would recite or read verses and offer simple prayers. On Sundays, they were not allowed to play games or read the comics in the newspaper.

The strict discipline in their home probably made Billy Frank a little more serious than some children, but it did not break his spirit or drain his energy. He loved to play practical jokes. He managed to stay out of trouble by being so good-natured. After school, he would play one of his favorite tricks. The Graham children rode a school bus. When they got off, Billy Frank would turn off the valve on the outside of the gas tank. The bus would start down the road, but sputter to a stop as if out of gas. The bus driver had to get off and turn the valve back on. He knew Billy Frank had done it. Years later, he said, "You couldn't get mad at the skinny so-and-so."

A classmate agreed. "He just liked everybody so enthusiastically that everybody had to like him. It was just this lovable feeling that he seemed to have for everybody. You couldn't resist him."

Because they lived in the country, the Graham children had few playmates. Billy Frank solved this problem by developing an addiction to reading when he was ten or eleven. He read about Tarzan, then acted out the stories in the woods, usually casting his brother and sisters as obedient monkeys. He read about cowboys and explorers. He even read a long book about the Roman Empire. He especially liked to read biographies of preachers and stories of brave missionaries in faraway lands. He would read in the hayloft of the barn, in his cluttered upstairs bedroom, or lying on his back in the middle of the living room floor with his legs propped up on a chair. As he read, he would chew his fingernails to the quick. The books fed his appetite for learning about people and places. But all that reading didn't make him a good student.

Billy Frank soon went to work on the family dairy farm. He was up at two-thirty or three o'clock to milk the cows. After school he had to haul and pitch hay to feed the cows. Then it was time to milk the cows again. He soon became the fastest milker on the farm, not because he liked milking, but because he wanted to get back to the house and to his books. During the hot, humid summers, he worked in the fields.

After he became a teenager Billy Frank still liked books, but he liked baseball and girls even better. For several years he spent most of his spare time on the baseball field, hoping he would someday be able to play big-league ball. But he wasn't good enough—especially at hitting.

He was more successful with the girls. His sister Catherine recalled that "he was in love with a different girl every day. He really did like the girls. And they liked him."

Like many teenage boys, Billy Frank was as unfinished as a young giraffe. His body seemed almost too spindly to support his large head. His broad smile and bright blue eyes gave him an appearance that, if not yet handsome, was certainly appealing. But his main appeal was that his father let him drive the family car. In those days, having a car was much better than looking like a football player.

Later, as a grown man, he admitted that he enjoyed spending time with girls but insisted that his relationships never went "in any way beyond kissing. Our parents expected us to be clean and never doubted that we would be. They trusted us and made us want to live up to their confidence."

In those days, it was common for a group of churches, or even just a group of local Christians, to invite a preacher to visit their city and hold a "revival" that would stir ("revive") people to become better Christians. Those attending would be encouraged to come forward at the end of the service to accept Jesus as their Savior.

These revivals lasted for weeks, even months, with preaching every night. They were held in churches or auditoriums or tents. Sometimes they were held in temporary buildings known as "tabernacles" that were torn down after the revival was over.

When Billy Frank was in high school, a preacher named Mordecai Ham came to Charlotte. The Grahams did not attend for the first week. Then a man who worked for Billy's father took a truckful of young people to the service. Billy Frank agreed to go. His parents started attending at about the same time, and the revival became the family's major evening activity for the next two months.

Each night, as many as 4,000 people filled the tin-roofed, unpainted pine tabernacle. The old preacher talked about their sins. Billy Frank was frightened, but he was also fascinated. "This man would stand up there and point his finger at you and name all the sins you had committed," he said years later. "It made you think your mother had been talking to him."

Billy Frank, about 1935.

To avoid having Ham look at him that way, Billy Frank joined the choir, even though he was a poor singer. He met two boys, Grady and T. W. Wilson, who had done the same thing for the same reason. The friendship that grew out of the experiences they shared on those cool fall evenings would last for the rest of their lives.

Each night at the end of the sermon, the preacher would urge those who wanted to become Christians or who wanted to ask for forgiveness of sins to come to the front of the tabernacle while the choir and congregation sang an "invitation hymn." Billy Frank had been learning Scripture verses and attending church all his life. He probably never imagined he wasn't a true Christian. But Mordecai Ham's preaching convinced him that he had not fully surrendered his life to Christ.

So one night Billy Frank and his friend Grady Wilson both "went forward" during that hymn. Many people who make this decision are filled with great emotion. Billy Frank was not. He later admitted that he had wondered if he should have felt something more dramatic, but he knew he was sincere. "I didn't have any tears," he remembered. "I didn't have any emotion. I didn't hear any thunder, there was no lightning. I didn't feel all worked up. But right there, I made my decision for Christ. It was as simple as that, and as conclusive."

Some people may have thought Billy Frank's experience was shallow. But he never did. "I knew something was different. I began to want to tell others what had happened to me. I began to want to read the Bible and pray. I began to memorize hymns."

As a sign of being more mature, he dropped his second name. He thought Billy Frank sounded too juvenile—like Sonny, Buddy, or Junior.

His friends Grady and T. W. Wilson announced that they intended to enter the ministry. Billy didn't think about becoming a preacher, yet he was fascinated by evangelists like Mordecai Ham and others who visited Charlotte and sometimes stayed with his family. He would listen to their sermons, thrill at their stories, and imitate their preaching in front of a mirror. But the thought of becoming one of them was still a long way off.

College Boy

Even though Billy was not a particularly good student, he expected to attend college when he finished high school. His mother wanted him to go to Wheaton College in Illinois, a conservative religious school she had read about. But it was too expensive and too far away from North Carolina. The family could not afford to send him there. Billy's father didn't think college was necessary. He wanted his son to stay home and help with the farm.

While they were trying to figure out what to do, one of the most famous preachers in the South, a man named Bob Jones, came to Charlotte to preach. Billy was a senior in high school.

Bob Jones was well-known for believing he was always right. He did not like anyone to disagree with him. He had founded Bob Jones College, a small school in

Tennessee that already had a reputation for being extremely strict. Frank Graham thought his son could use some hardheaded discipline and agreed that Billy could attend Bob Jones College if he wanted to. It cost about a dollar a day to go to that school. Billy wasn't sure, but when his friend T. W. Wilson attended the college for a semester and came home with glowing reports, Billy decided it might be okay. He was also encouraged to attend by a young evangelist he admired, Jimmie Johnson, who had attended Bob Jones College. Johnson was handsome, knew the Bible well, and was a terrific preacher. He told Billy the college was a wonderful place. That was all Billy needed. Bob Jones would be his college.

During the summer of 1936, after he graduated from high school and before he started college, Billy worked as a Fuller Brush salesman. He went from house to house selling all kinds of brushes—hairbrushes, toothbrushes, shower brushes, and many others. Billy turned out to be an excellent salesman. He worked hard. He prayed as he walked between houses. And he really believed in the product.

Later on he would say, "Sincerity is the biggest part of selling anything, including the Christian plan of salvation. Selling those brushes became a cause to me. I felt that every family ought to have Fuller brushes." At the end of the summer, Billy had sold more brushes than any other Fuller salesman in North or South Carolina.

That summer, Billy and the Wilson brothers happened to be working in the same town where Jimmie Johnson was holding a revival. One Sunday, Jimmie talked Billy and Grady into going with him to the city jail to hold a service for the prisoners. Neither boy had ever been inside a jail. The sights and sounds and smells made a strong impression on them.

Jimmie Johnson gave a short sermon, then he introduced Billy as a young man who wanted to tell the prisoners what Jesus had done for him. Billy was surprised. He didn't know what to say but felt he had to say something. He started by saying, "I'm glad to see so many of you out this afternoon," which was a strange thing to say to people in jail. He told the prisoners that he had not taken religion too seriously while he was growing up. But since he had been converted, he said, "Jesus changed my life! He gave me peace and joy! He can give you peace and joy! He will forgive your sins as he forgave mine if you'll only let him in your heart! Jesus died so he could take your sins on his shoulders."

It was short. It could hardly be called a sermon. But that basic message would be the central theme of Billy Graham's preaching for more than seventy years.

Bob Jones College was difficult for Billy. In addition to a packed schedule of classes, students attended chapel every day, vesper services at dusk, and regular devotions in their dormitories at night. Boys and girls were not allowed to touch each other, not even to hold hands. The only dates they could have were fifteen minutes of conversation, once a week, in a parlor with a chaperone nearby. Students who did not like the strict rules were warned to obey signs that said, "Griping Not Tolerated."

Billy tried to fit in. But he had never learned to study in high school, and he couldn't keep up with his classes. He also didn't like all the regulations. He suffered from allergies. He got the flu. He lost weight.

When he went home for Christmas, a Charlotte doctor suggested that he might be better off in a warmer climate. An evangelist who was visiting in the Graham home recommended the Florida Bible Institute in Temple Terrace, a suburb of Tampa. Morrow Graham convinced her husband that they should visit Florida for a few days over the Christmas holidays to take a look at that new little college.

Billy fell in love with Florida, with its warm climate and lakes and palm trees and flowers. It was a sharp contrast to the cold unfriendliness at Bob Jones College.

When Billy returned to college after the holidays, he told other students how much he liked the Florida school. Dr. Jones heard about it. He called Billy in to warn him against such talk. "Billy," he said, "if you throw your life away at a little country Bible school, the chances are you'll never be heard of. At best, all you could amount to would be a poor country Baptist preacher somewhere out in the sticks."

Even though Dr. Jones was angry, he knew that Billy had potential. "You have a voice that appeals," Jones said. "God can use that voice of yours. He can use it mightily."

Billy sat there listening with his head down, biting his nails. It was hard for him to challenge anyone in authority.

But before long, Billy got sick again. This time he told his parents he wanted to transfer to the Florida school. A few days later, the Grahams loaded up their gray Plymouth and took their son to Tampa.

Florida Bible Institute was in a building that had once been a country club and hotel that had gone out of business. The founder and president of the school, W. T. Watson, was able to buy the property cheap. He decided to use part of the property for his school and to keep the rest as a hotel and golf course. That had several advantages. Christian families could go there on vacation, knowing it would be a wholesome place. Famous evangelists and other church leaders could visit for several weeks at a time, teaching classes and preaching in return for free room and food. And students could help pay their way by working as waiters, busboys, dishwashers, maids, and caddies.

Billy loved his new environment. He swam and canoed in the swampy river that bordered the campus. He played tennis about like he played baseball—not very well. And he spent as much time as he could on the golf course, learning the game he would play for many years. That first year, he said, "I was really just a glorified tourist who was taking a few Bible courses."

At Florida Bible Institute, Billy got to meet famous evangelists, teachers, pastors, radio preachers, and missionaries. Whenever they came to visit, he spent as much time around them as he could. He served their tables, he polished their shoes, he caddied for them, he carried their bags, he had his picture taken with them, and he wrote home to tell his mother how much he wanted to be like this one or that one.

He studied their strengths and weaknesses, determined to find some way he too could be a great servant of the Lord and the church. The founder of the school remembered that "Billy always wanted to do something big. He didn't know exactly what yet, but he couldn't wait just to do something big, whatever it was."

Eventually, Billy decided. He told his mother in a letter, "I think the Lord is calling me to the ministry, and if he does it will be in the field of evangelism."

3

The Boy Preacher

Billy's most important friend and counselor during his Florida days was the Reverend John Minder, the dean of the Institute. The dean saw Billy as a young man of special promise and did what he could to encourage him. One Sunday, Minder invited Billy to come with him to visit a friend who was a preacher in a nearby town. It was a setup. When the friend invited the dean to preach that evening, he smiled and said, "Billy's preaching tonight."

Billy had never preached a sermon. But he had thought about it. A lot. In fact, he had secretly practiced four sermons that he had read in a book. That night, before a congregation of no more than twenty-five or thirty rural Baptists whose dogs scratched around outside the little wooden church, Billy Graham preached his first real sermon.

Actually, he preached his first four real sermons. He

had thought that any one of them would take at least half an hour, but he was so nervous that he finished all four in less than eight minutes. Billy thought he had been a miserable failure, but Dean Minder, who also was pastor of the Tampa Gospel Tabernacle, soon invited Billy to become the youth director.

The rules at the Institute were strict, but not as strict as those at Bob Jones College. Billy began looking for girls he could date. He soon settled on a lively dark-haired beauty named Emily Cavanagh. Although he was only eighteen, he asked her to marry him. Emily thought Billy was admirable, fascinating, and lovable, but she hesitated. She probably thought they both were too young. Finally, she accepted his proposal, but a few weeks later she broke their engagement and started dating an older student who seemed headed for a successful career in the ministry.

Billy was devastated. He turned to prayer and the Scriptures for comfort. He also became more serious about deciding what to do with his life. Night after sleepless night, for three or four hours at a time, he walked the streets of the town or roamed nearby country roads, praying aloud as he walked.

Then, around midnight one evening, as he returned to the campus he got down on his knees beside the eighteenth green of the golf course. "All right, Lord, if you want me, you've got me. I'll be what you want me to be and I'll go where you want me to go."

He was finally sure that God was calling him to preach.

Billy preached occasionally at the Gospel Tabernacle and at little country churches, but he also found more unusual places to preach. He held outdoor services at an empty racetrack. He preached on street corners, which often did not turn out too well. Once, when he started preaching against sin at the doorway of a saloon on one of Tampa's roughest streets, an angry bartender knocked him down and shoved him face-first into the mud. On Sunday afternoons, he preached at a jail and in the evening preached again at the Tampa Trailer Park, which had room for a thousand trailers and often provided an audience of several hundred people on vacation. He was on his way.

In the summer of 1938, Billy held his first revival, at the East Palatka Baptist Church. Baptists believe that a saved person should be baptized by complete immersion in water soon after accepting Jesus as their Savior. They require it for church membership. Because Billy had grown up in a Presbyterian church, he had been sprinkled in baptism as an infant shortly after his birth. When the leaders of the East Palatka church learned that Billy had never been baptized by immersion, they persuaded him to join a group of people who were being baptized in a nearby lake as a result of hearing him preach.

Several months later, Billy was ordained as an evangelist by the St. John's Baptist Association of Northern Florida. He would always admire and have many associations with Presbyterians, but from then on he considered himself to be a Baptist.

Like Billy, most of the young men at Florida Bible

Institute intended to become preachers. Some of them probably had as much or more natural talent than he did. What made Billy different was that he poured every possible ounce of his talent and effort into his preaching. He read the sermons of other men, often memorizing them entirely. Nearly every afternoon when classes ended, he took a book of sermons and went into an old shed next to his dormitory and preached to oil cans and lawnmowers. Or he paddled a canoe to a lonely spot on the river and called on snakes and alligators and tree stumps to repent of their sins and accept Jesus.

One afternoon, Dean Watson heard him preaching loudly in his dormitory room. He looked through the door and saw his own four-year-old son perched on Billy's dresser, serving as the audience for the young preacher's sermon.

Billy talked so fast and waved his arms so much while he preached that his friends began to call him "The Preaching Windmill." Even his mother, who seldom criticized him about anything, admitted that his preaching during those days was "awfully loud."

Billy was willing to practice his sermons before an empty space, but when the time came to face a live audience, he wanted those seats full. He soon learned the power of advertising. He distributed fliers that described him as "Dynamic Youth Evangelist Billy Graham — a Great Gospel Preacher at 21." Another, even more grand, was titled "Billy Graham, One of America's Outstanding Young Evangelists." He once ordered a thousand fliers to distribute in a town that had only two hundred people.

Because of his success as a preacher, Billy's classmates elected him president of the senior class. He was named the outstanding evangelist at the school. With the experience he already had, it would have been easy to keep on holding revivals in the area, perhaps becoming as successful and well-known as his friend Jimmie Johnson. But the Institute did not teach much more than the Bible and practical instructions for preachers and other church workers.

Billy realized there were great gaps in his education. He decided to accept a remarkable offer he had received a few months earlier from two visitors who had stayed at the hotel. They had heard Billy preach at the Gospel Tabernacle and they were impressed, but felt he needed better education. One was the brother of the president of Wheaton College. The other was the brother of the president of Wheaton's board of trustees.

They told Billy he should go to Wheaton.

"That's what my mother wanted," he said, "but it's too expensive."

They offered to pay for his first year at Wheaton and to use their influence to get him a scholarship for the other years.

Billy saw their offer as an answer to prayer. After another summer of revivals, he set out for the widely admired Chicago-area school and opportunities that would eventually take him around the world.

4

Ruth

Wheaton College was a deeply religious school. Its motto was "For Christ and His Kingdom." But it was also a real college and not just a Bible school. Because it gave Billy almost no credit for the courses he had taken at either Bob Jones College or Florida Bible Institute, he had to enroll as a freshman, even though he was almost twenty-two years old. He was starting all over.

His bright clothes, high-top shoes, and southern accent caused some people to think he was just a simple country boy. But his age and his experience as an evangelist helped him become a well-known and admired campus figure.

Even though his basic school expenses had been taken care of, Billy needed spending money. He found a job working for another student who hauled luggage and furniture in a battered old yellow pickup. That student was preparing to be a missionary in China and he introduced Billy to Ruth Bell, a sophomore who had grown up in China as the daughter of a Presbyterian medical missionary. Billy fell in love. He wrote to his mother to tell her about this new girl he met.

Although Ruth's father, Dr. L. Nelson Bell, took good care of his family, like most missionaries they did not have much extra money. When Ruth entered Wheaton in 1937, her "dress-up" wardrobe contained only one good black dress, a blue tweed suit she had picked up at a street bazaar in Chicago, and some dime-store pearls. Even so, her vivacious beauty, a young lifetime of unusual experiences on the mission field, and her practice of waking up at 5:00 a.m. for prayer and Bible reading made her the prize catch of her class.

Billy intended to catch her.

Ruth barely noticed him when they were introduced. But not long afterward, he impressed her with his prayer at an informal church meeting. "I had never heard anyone pray like that before," she said. "I sensed that here was a man that knew God in a very unusual way." When Billy finally worked up the courage to ask Ruth to go with him to a performance of Handel's *Messiah*, she accepted. After the concert and a slow, snowy walk to a professor's house for tea, he wrote home again, announcing that he planned to marry this new girl who reminded him so much of his mother.

The Grahams made no wedding plans. Billy's younger sister Jean recalled, "He had fallen in love so many times, we didn't pay much attention to him."

Ruth talked only to God about her plans. "If you let me serve you with that man, I'd consider it the greatest privilege in my life," she prayed.

Ruth's and Billy's childhoods could not have been more different. He had read books about faraway lands. She grew up about as far away from North Carolina as it was possible to get. He had heard sermons on the wickedness of playing cards and using profanity. She had walked to school alongside dirty streams where dogs ate the bodies of infants killed by parents who didn't want them. He arose at 2:30 a.m. to milk cows. Ruth often still lay awake at that hour, unable to sleep because of the noise from gunfire and bombs or from fear of the rats and scorpions they could not keep out of their home.

Despite these differences, Billy and Ruth had much in common. Billy had dreamed of playing baseball in the big leagues. Ruth's father loved baseball. In fact, he had signed a contract with a Baltimore Orioles farm team shortly before he decided to become a medical missionary. Like the Grahams, the Bells were Presbyterians who prayed regularly with their children and expected them to learn large sections of scripture by memory.

Ruth's religion had taken a serious turn far earlier than Billy's. By the time she was twelve, she was talking about a career as a missionary to Tibet. She prayed regularly that God would allow her to die as a martyr.

Her older sister, Rosa, heard these prayers and would quietly pray, "Please don't listen to her, God. She's just a little girl and doesn't know what she's saying."

Billy's and Ruth's courtship was peculiar. Billy seemed to doubt he deserved or could win Ruth's love. He would ask her for a date, then not contact her for several weeks. When he would ask for another date, he also asked if he was embarrassing her by taking her out too often.

She was intrigued by this young man with an uncommon determination to do God's will, but since he couldn't seem to make up his mind, she decided to date other students. That worked. Billy said, "Either you date just me, or you can date everybody *but* me!"

After that, they began to go out on a regular basis, usually to some service where he preached. He impressed her with his bold presentation of the Gospel, but she later confessed she thought his preaching was too loud and too fast.

As Billy grew more confident about their relationship, he began to act more like the "man in charge," the way his own father had acted. He told Ruth what to eat and sat across from her until she obeyed. He insisted she get more exercise and personally put her through a rigorous program of calisthenics. She admitted to her parents that Bill (she never called him Billy) "isn't awfully easy to love because of his sternness and unwavering stand on certain issues." But when he assured her that he did what he did because he loved her, she stopped resisting him.

By the time she came to Wheaton, Ruth no longer wanted to be a martyr, but she still dreamed of being a missionary to Tibet. Billy respected this, but tried to convince her that the highest role a woman could fill was that of wife and mother. They read the Bible and prayed that God would lead them in the right direction.

When God gave them no clear answer, Billy decided to proceed without it. At the end of the spring semester in 1941, just before they parted for the summer, he asked Ruth to marry him. She did not respond.

A few weeks later, she wrote to him. She told him that she believed their relationship was "of the Lord" and would be pleased to become his wife. She didn't see an easy life ahead. She acknowledged to her parents that "to be with Bill in evangelistic work will not be easy. There will be little financial backing, lots of obstacles and criticism, and no earthly glory whatsoever, but I knew I wouldn't have peace till I yielded my will to the Lord and decided to marry Bill."

They set their wedding date for August 1943, after both had finished college.

Billy began to preach at small churches in the area and soon became the regular preacher at Wheaton's United

Billy and Ruth on their wedding day, August 13, 1943, in Montreat Presbyterian Church, Montreat, North Carolina.

Billy Graham Evangelistic Association

Gospel Tabernacle. Early in 1943, he was invited to become the pastor of a small Baptist church in nearby Western Springs, Illinois. Billy accepted the offer without consulting Ruth.

She was offended. She thought he should have been thoughtful enough to talk with her about such an important decision even if he was going to be the head of their family.

After their wedding and a seven-day honeymoon in Blowing Rock, North Carolina, Ruth got sick on the trip back to Western Springs. Billy had agreed to preach at a church in Ohio on their way back. It was just a routine service. He could have called to tell them he needed to stay at the bedside of his brand-new bride, which they surely would have understood. Instead, Billy checked Ruth into a local hospital and kept the appointment. To make her feel better, he sent her a telegram and a box of candy. She felt hurt at this apparent lack of concern for her condition and her feelings, but she soon learned that nothing came before preaching on her husband's list of priorities. This would not be the last time he would leave a hospital bed (including his own) or miss key moments of sorrow or celebration because of a promise to preach.

Billy helped the Western Springs church grow, but he didn't like being tied down to one place. He wanted to reach more people than he could in one little church. A man who realized this most clearly was Torrey Johnson, the pastor of a thriving church in Chicago. Johnson produced a popular Sunday evening radio program, *Songs in the Night,* aired over a powerful radio station that could be heard far from Chicago. One day he asked Billy to take his place on the program.

Billy accepted. He also convinced the Western Springs church to accept the challenge of raising the $150 to pay for each week's program.

Next, Billy convinced George Beverly Shea, a popular religious singer, to become the show's primary musical performer. Beginning in January 1944, from 10:30 to 11:15 on Sunday evenings, "Bev" Shea would sing hymns and gospel songs in his rich, deep voice. Billy, sitting at a table outlined in colored lights to provide a dramatic setting for the studio audience, offered brief meditations. He talked about how the Christian message related to common problems and situations, about the loneliness of families separated by war—World War II was still going on—about the need for courage and confidence in the face of danger and fear, and about the importance of living a clean life.

Back in Charlotte, Frank and Morrow Graham would sit in their car, which had a stronger radio than the one in their home, and strain through the static to hear their son's familiar voice. "Imagine!" they would say. "That's our Billy Frank."

5

Youth for Christ

From 1941 to 1945, the United States was heavily in-
volved in World War II, fighting the Germans in
Europe and the Japanese in the Pacific. It was the worst
war in human history. The war was a serious threat
to the freedom of people in many countries, including
Americans.

Billy wanted to help. He enlisted in the Army to become a chaplain, to be a minister to men and women in
the military. But before he was able to go through the
training, he got a severe case of the mumps and had to
stay in bed for six weeks. At times, his temperature rose
to 105 degrees. Doctors were afraid he might die. He lost
so much weight and was so weak that he was unable to
serve under the hard conditions of war, so he decided to
do what he could to help members of the military and
other young people in the United States.

Ministers in several large cities had begun holding programs on Saturday nights to offer young people, especially young soldiers and sailors stationed far from home, some wholesome entertainment, patriotic fervor, and religious encouragement. Billy's friend Torrey Johnson attended some of these rallies and decided to start a similar program in Chicago. He rented a 3,000-seat auditorium and invited Billy to speak at the first rally in May 1944.

It was by far the largest audience Billy had ever faced. He walked back and forth behind the curtain, suffering what he called "the worst case of stage fright of my life." But even though he was scared, he was prepared. He did a terrific job, and many people accepted the invitation at the end of his sermon.

These programs continued all summer. They were so successful that Torrey Johnson convinced Billy to resign from the Western Springs church and become a full-time worker for a new organization, Youth for Christ International. In this role, Billy continued to preach at rallies, but he mainly traveled around the country showing ministers and youth leaders how to establish Youth for Christ organizations in their cities. During 1945, Billy visited forty-seven of the forty-eight states and flew at least 135,000 miles, the most of any civilian passenger on United Airlines.

Ruth was left at home. She understood that the life of an evangelist would take her husband away from her much of the time. She was pregnant with their first child and decided to move from Illinois.

The war had forced her parents out of China. They had moved to Montreat, North Carolina, a pretty little town that had a Presbyterian college and conference center and that served as a retirement community for Presbyterian ministers.

Ruth packed up their few possessions and moved in with her parents. They taught her the skills of home-making and helped ease the loneliness she felt during Billy's long absences. They were also there to share important moments. When Billy's and Ruth's first child, Virginia (always called "GiGi"), was born on September 21, 1945, Billy was away on a preaching trip.

Ruth missed her husband so much that she sometimes slept with one of his sport coats beside her. But she knew he was doing what God wanted him to do. She told people, "I'd rather have a little of Bill than a lot of any other man."

The Youth for Christ programs were designed to show young people that Christianity did not have to be drab and dismal. Their advertisements promised "Old-Fashioned Truth for Up-to-Date Youth" that was "Geared to the Times, but Anchored to the Rock." The Rock, of course, was Jesus.

The dynamic young men who led this movement, which was spreading all over the nation, wore colorful suits and sport coats, bright hand-painted ties, and gaudy bow ties. Some of the bow ties even lit up. The programs included choirs and quartets and trios and soloists, Bible quizzes, and patriotic and spiritual testimonies by famous athletes, entertainers, and military heroes. Sometimes they featured magicians and ventriloquists. They even had a horse. They would ask the horse how many apostles Jesus had. The horse would kneel in front of a cross and tap his hoof twelve times.

Preaching a message while serving for Youth for Christ.

Billy said, "We used every modern means to catch the attention of the unconverted — and then we punched them right between the eyes with the Gospel."

The most spectacular program of all occurred in Soldier Field in Chicago on Memorial Day, 1945. Seventy thousand young people packed the giant stadium. A 300-piece band accompanied a 5,000-voice choir that led the audience in singing "The Star-Spangled Banner." A world-champion miler ran an exhibition race. A young man from the University of Virginia told how Christ had helped him become a national college boxing champion. Four hundred nurses arranged in the shape of a cross marched down the field as the band played "The Battle Hymn of the Republic." Hundreds of high school students placed a wreath on a platform crowned by a large blue star—families who had a son or daughter in the war displayed a banner with a blue star in their window.

At the end of the service, all the lights in the stadium went out. A strong spotlight circled the stands, falling on the crowd. The spotlight was to remind them that they are to be "the light of the world."

Then, during the closing prayer, a huge sign, hidden until that moment, proclaimed the heart of the evangelical message: "JESUS SAVES."

In 1946, just a few months after the long and terrible war finally ended, Billy and a small group of young preachers flew to England to establish Youth for Christ organizations there. That country was still climbing out of the rubble of war, still frequently dark from blackouts because of poor electricity service, and still lacking all but the most basic things needed to survive. The sight of these exuberant, backslapping young Americans in bright-colored suits and sport coats and rainbow ties scandalized some people but delighted others.

A London minister described them as "like a breath from heaven in a suffocated time, men who brought brightness in the midst of all our darkness."

Once, when Billy and his friends changed into more conservative clothes for dinner, their hosts insisted, "Please go up and change your clothes again. We want you just like you were."

Billy returned to England for several months in the fall of 1946. This time, he invited Cliff and Billie Barrows to serve as his musical team. Cliff was an excellent evangelist himself, but they worked together so well

Bev Shea, Cliff Barrows, and Billy served together for nearly sixty years. Here they lead the final crusade in New York in 2005.

on that trip that Cliff decided to stay with Billy as his song leader and choir director. Nearly sixty years later, at the great gathering you read about in the prologue of this book, that little team of three—Billy Graham, George Beverly Shea, and Cliff Barrows—was still together as friends and coworkers for Christ.

That winter of 1946–47 was bitterly cold, the worst in decades. Economic conditions were still extremely bad. To save money while in England, the little group frequently rented rooms in homes rather than in hotels. Billy and another Youth for Christ evangelist, George Wilson, often slept in the same bed, fully dressed and wearing shawls over their heads to keep warm. On occasion, they spoke in stone churches so cold and damp that fog kept them from seeing part of the congregation in the back of the sanctuary.

These hardships did not dampen their spirits or cool their enthusiasm. During those six months, Billy spoke at 360 meetings throughout England. In some places, local ministers opposed their efforts. The ministers said they didn't need help from "America's surplus saints." Instead of arguing with them, Billy visited those who were most critical of his efforts. He would pray with them and explain that his only interest was in helping them further the cause of Christ in their country. Again and again, he melted the hearts of the men who had opposed him.

One critic said, "I ended up wanting to hug the twenty-seven-year-old boy. This fine man made me love him and his Lord."

As Billy spent time with veteran preachers in England, he learned how their faith had helped them deal with the hard circumstances of the war. They taught him how to become closer to God and to preach in a more thoughtful and effective way.

There were many dedicated and talented evangelists in Youth for Christ, but Billy was the most successful. He soon began thinking about an independent ministry that would hold longer revivals for everyone, not just for young people. The first big revival he held, in the fall of 1947, was in his hometown of Charlotte, North Carolina. Once again, he was afraid he would fail.

He convinced the people who had invited him to conduct an extensive advertising campaign. In addition to billboards and bumper stickers and posters, airplanes dropped leaflets and pulled sky banners advertising the revival. Volunteers made 5,000 telephone calls a day, inviting people to the services.

AP/Wide World Photos

Billy, second from right, kneels in prayer on the White House Lawn on July 14, 1950, asking divine aid for President Truman in his handling of the Korean crisis. Graham had just finished a meeting with the President. With him are, left to right, Jerry Beavan, Clifford Barrows, and Grady Wilson.

Billy also used some of the musical and variety acts that appeared on Youth for Christ programs. And, of course, he prepared his sermons very carefully. As it usually does, planning and hard work paid off. The revival was a great success, attracting 42,000 people over eighteen services.

Encouraged by this and other successes, Billy soon resigned his full-time position with Youth for Christ. But he remained on the organization's board of directors and continued to support its activities.

In later years, whenever he would hold a revival in cities throughout America, some of the men who helped him most were those he had met during his travels for Youth for Christ.

Billy had learned the value of thorough preparation and lots of publicity.

At age thirty, Billy Graham was ready for new challenges.

6

The Canvas Cathedral

World War II ended in 1945. In the years right after the war, Americans experienced widespread religious revival. All over the country, church membership was rising. New churches were being built. People were buying millions of Bibles and other religious books.

Many men decided to become full-time evangelists and hold revivals around the country. Most were sincere and honest, but some were not. And they did things that caused people to be suspicious of all evangelists. Billy knew this and wanted to make sure that he and the men who worked with him did nothing to bring shame on the church or its ministers. So, in November 1948, while he was holding a revival in Modesto, California, he called the members of his little "team"—Cliff Barrows, Bev Shea, and Grady Wilson—to his hotel room.

"God has brought us to this point," he said. "Maybe he is preparing us for something larger. Let's try to think of all the things we can that have been a problem for evangelists in the past and let's come back together and talk about it and pray about it and ask God to guard us from those problems."

Later in the afternoon, when they got back together, it turned out that they had all made almost the same list of problems. One was money. At that time, and often still today, evangelists did not draw a regular salary. They depended on the offerings that were taken up during their services. It was easy to get greedy and pretend that they needed more money than they really did, so that people would feel sorry for them and give them money even when they couldn't afford to. Besides that, some evangelists would leave town without paying the bills for their hotel or other expenses such as advertising. Billy and his team decided they would never emphasize the offering. They also decided that a committee of local people would be in charge of using the donations to pay all the bills and then determine how much the evangelists and Billy's team would receive.

They also knew that sexual temptation can be powerful, for preachers just like everyone else. They made rules to keep themselves out of trouble. From then on, they would never be alone in a restaurant or a car with a woman other than their wife, sister, or daughter. If they needed to talk with a woman in an office, they would always keep the door open so that no one could think they were behaving improperly.

Some evangelists had also caused trouble in churches by criticizing the local preacher to make themselves look better and perhaps cause people to give them more money. Billy and his friends agreed they would always cooperate with local ministers as much as possible and urge people to be faithful to their own churches, rather than to regard the traveling evangelist as their new pastor.

The last problem they pledged to avoid was exaggerating their success when they reported on their revivals. (Some evangelists had been accused of counting arms and legs instead of heads when they talked about how many people had attended their services.) Billy and his team would try to be as accurate as possible when they talked about the size of their crowds or the number of people who had responded to the invitation. In fact, if the police, reporters, or people who were in charge of the buildings where they preached made an estimate they knew was too low, Billy would just accept that number rather than argue about it.

When organizations or individuals, such as political candidates, make a public statement of their policies and goals, it is often called a "manifesto." These simple decisions that helped Billy Graham and his organization avoid serious problems for the rest of his long ministry became known as the Modesto Manifesto. It was adopted by many other ministers who wanted to avoid trouble.

Over his long career, Billy Graham held many, many revivals, which he came to call "crusades." Nearly all of

The Los Angeles evangelistic campaign, Fall 1949, was held in the "Canvas Cathedral" and was the beginning of Billy's national press coverage and recognition.

them were successful, but some stood out as especially important. The first really big crusade was in Los Angeles in 1949. They rented a huge circus tent that could hold six thousand people. Posters, billboards, newspaper ads, and radio commercials invited people to visit "The Canvas Cathedral with the Steeple of Light." The "steeple" was a bright spotlight that could be seen for miles.

Like the Youth for Christ rallies, the services included special music and testimonies, but they were geared more for adults. There were no magicians, ventriloquists, or foot-tapping horses. Cliff Barrows led the singing. The hymns were familiar so people would feel comfortable. Billy told reporters, "We believe it is a spiritual service. We don't believe it is a concert or a show."

Still, because of Billy's dynamic preaching, the services were much more exciting than those in most churches.

The pulpit, which stood in the middle of a long wooden platform, was painted to look like a giant open Bible. Billy began most of his sermons while standing behind that pulpit, but he didn't stay there long. He stayed in motion, using a lapel microphone that gave him freedom to stalk back and forth across the platform. Cliff had to make sure Billy didn't get tangled up in the long cord—wireless microphones hadn't been invented yet. During a sermon, Billy would often walk at least a mile. That bothered some people, but it kept attention riveted on him. It made listeners in all sections of that big tent feel he was speaking directly to them at least part of the time.

Just as he had done when he was at Florida Bible Institute, Billy practiced his sermons over and over. He had learned what worked best. He would look straight at people while preaching. And he'd speak in different ways to hold their attention—fast, then slow; loud, then soft. "It's that difference in delivery that holds them," he said. He would shape his hands into pistols and use his arms like a sword, firing and slashing at sin. Over and over again, as he held the limp Bible high overhead or brought his hands down like lightning to where it lay open on the pulpit, he would warn the audience to listen to his words, saying, "The Bible says ...!"

In those days, revivals might be planned for two or three weeks, but if the crowds were good and many people were responding to the invitation, the sponsors could decide to keep going. After three weeks of tent meetings in Los Angeles, just when it looked like it might be about time to stop, several remarkable things happened.

Stuart Hamblen, a cowboy singer with a popular radio show, had been coming to the services. He had grown up in a Christian home, but had stopped going to church and had become a heavy drinker. He had listened to Billy preach and felt the sermons were aimed directly at him. One night, in the middle of the night, Hamblen showed up at Billy's hotel room. He told Billy he wanted to come back to the Lord. After that, Hamblen began using his radio program to urge people to attend Billy's revival. That helped build the crowds. But something bigger was about to happen.

One night, without warning, a cluster of reporters and photographers were waiting for Billy when he arrived at the tent for the service. He was puzzled, even a bit frightened. "What happened?" he asked a reporter.

Back then, news bulletins were sent to machines at newspapers that printed the words on a narrow strip of paper. The reporter showed Billy a torn strip with just two words on it. It had been sent by William Randolph Hearst, a powerful man who owned newspapers and magazines in cities across America. The message said, "Puff Graham." That meant the Hearst newspapers would give Billy Graham lots of publicity. Billy never knew why Hearst did this, but it definitely worked.

As soon as the Hearst papers started printing front-page stories about the Billy Graham revival, other newspapers and magazines did the same thing. The revival stretched from three weeks to eight weeks. Crowds grew so large that the tent was expanded to hold nine thousand people. Sometimes the tent would be full hours before the service started. Movie stars and other celebrities came every night. An Olympic champion, a war hero, and a gangster were all converted, bringing even greater publicity. Suddenly, whatever Billy Graham said on any subject was likely to find its way into newspapers. By the time the revival ended, attendance had totaled nearly 350,000 people. About seven hundred churches had helped in some way.

Before the 1949 Los Angeles revival, Billy Graham was well-known in evangelical churches. At the end of his two months in the Canvas Cathedral, he had become one of the most famous men in America.

The Hour of Decision

Early in 1950, Billy held a revival in Boston that shook up that dignified old city. At a press conference before the revival began, a reporter asked Billy how much money he expected to "rake in" from the offerings at the services.

Billy had a perfect reply. Just before the press conference, a bellhop had handed him a telegram, which he read and stuck in his pocket. Now he showed the telegram to the reporter, saying, "Sir, if I were interested in making money, I would take advantage of something like this."

The telegram was from a movie producer who was offering Billy $250,000 to star in Hollywood films. The reporter saw that the telegram was genuine. From then on, Billy got friendly front-page coverage in all five Boston newspapers.

Billy captivated Boston with some of the most colorful preaching of his entire career, drawing much more on his imagination than on the Bible. Here's how he described heaven: "We are going to sit around the fireplace and have parties and the angels will wait on us and we'll drive down the golden streets in a yellow Cadillac convertible. I hope to be able to sing, play the trombone and violin, and play football and baseball as well as the best."

When he preached on the familiar story of Daniel in the lion's den, Billy described it this way: "Daniel walks in. He's not afraid. He looks the first big cat in the eye and kicks him and says, 'Move over there, Leo. I want me a nice fat lion with a soft belly for a pillow, so I can get another good night's rest.'"

To describe his preaching, one reporter wrote, "He prowls like a panther... He becomes a haughty and sneering Roman, his head flies back arrogantly and his voice is harsh and gruff. He becomes a penitent sinner; his head bows, his eyes roll up in supplication, his voice cracks and quavers. He becomes an avenging angel; his arms rise up above his head and his long fingers snap out like talons. So perfect are the portrayals that his audience sits tense and fascinated as his sermons take on a vividness, a reality hard to describe."

Not everyone was fascinated. Ruth Graham was able to spend a few days in Boston while her parents took care of things back in Montreat. After hearing Billy preach that way, she told reporters, "As an actor, I'm afraid he is pretty much a ham. When he starts that kind of acting sermon, I usually start to squirm."

She told her husband, "Bill, Jesus didn't act out the gospel. He just preached it. I think that's all he has called you to do!"

That summer, Billy held another great crusade in Portland, Oregon. Because auditoriums in Boston had been too small to hold everyone who wanted to come, Billy convinced the sponsors in Portland to build a 12,000-seat wood-and-aluminum tabernacle the size of a football field. But even this wasn't big enough. The first service drew a crowd of well over 20,000 people. During the second week, 250,000 people tried to get in to hear Billy.

Something even more important than the crowds happened in Portland. Two men offered Billy a chance to preach on the national ABC radio network on Sunday afternoons. Most big cities had television stations, but not many people had television sets in their homes. Radio was still the best way to reach the most people.

Billy wanted to do the program. It would be the beginning of a national radio ministry. Every week, he could preach to thousands. But he was afraid the radio time would cost far more than he could afford to pay.

He didn't give up. He knelt by his bed in the hotel and prayed. He told God, "We don't have the money, but I would like to do it. I will need a sign from you. If I can raise $25,000 by midnight tonight, I will agree to start a radio program."

Then Billy had to figure out how he could ask the people at the revival for the money. He had pledged in Modesto that he would never beg for money. He would never push people to give. What could he say that wouldn't break that pledge?

He prayed.

At the crusade that night, he did not use high pressure on the congregation. He simply said, "A couple of men are here to see us about going on radio. The time is available; we can let the tobacco people have it, or we can take it for God. If you want to have a part in this, I'll be in the little room by the choir area after the service tonight."

The service went on longer than usual. But when it was over, hundreds of people stayed late and lined up to drop checks, bills, pledges, and even a few coins into a shoe box. They counted the money. Billy had $23,500.

The radio men were happy and excited until Billy reminded them, "I didn't ask for $23,500. I asked for $25,000."

The two men offered to make up the $1,500 difference, but Billy wouldn't accept their money. He said it would be wrong to think the money collected was a sign from God. "The Devil could give me $23,500."

Billy and his team went back to the hotel.

But God had a surprise waiting for them. The desk clerk had two envelopes waiting for them. One was from a Texas businessman with a check for $1,000 for the radio program. The other was from a person who had been at the crusade but didn't want to wait in line to contribute, so dropped his check off at the hotel. The check was for $500. The two checks totaled $1,500—the exact amount needed to bring the total to $25,000. To Billy

Graham, this was a clear sign God was calling him to a radio ministry.

Ruth suggested the title for the radio show— *The Hour of Decision*. The first program went on the air from Atlanta on November 5, 1950. In only five weeks, it was the most popular religious broadcast on radio. Within

Addressing a crowd at a religious rally in front of the U.S. Capitol Building in Washington, D.C., Feb. 3, 1952.

a year, it could be heard on nearly a thousand stations in the United States and other parts of the world. In 1951, Billy started a television version of the program, but it was never as successful as *The Hour of Decision* on radio. At about this time, Billy also began making movies. These told stories of people who were in trouble and what happened to them after they accepted Christ at a Billy Graham crusade.

In 1952, Billy held a crusade in Washington, D.C. The high point was the first religious service ever to be held on the steps of the Capitol. In spite of a steady rain, 40,000 people stood out in the open to hear Billy's message about Jesus.

That crusade in Washington was the beginning of Billy's friendships with many important political leaders. With their help, he traveled to South Korea, where American soldiers were at war with Communists from North Korea and China. The Pentagon, the headquarters of the United States Department of Defense, provided Billy with airplanes and jeeps that allowed him to meet with generals and soldiers throughout the area.

Billy and members of his team visited orphanages in South Korea set up by American soldiers to care for children whose parents and other family members had been killed in the war. He visited hospitals, some in tents, where wounded soldiers were being treated. He prayed for them. He saw terrible things: "men with their eyes shot out—their arms mutilated—gaping wounds in their sides and back—their skin charred by horrible burns. I wish every American could stand in the hospitals with me," he said. "They would have a new sense of the horror of war."

He also prayed for the Communist soldiers who were wounded and suffering. "Our God is not only the God of the Americans," he said, "but also of the Communists. I am convinced that we as Christians should pray daily for our Communist enemies."

Billy even spent several days at the battlefront. Flying through thick fog in small planes or helicopters, he was so close to enemy guns that exploding shells shook the aircraft several times. After landing at a tiny airstrip, Billy would put on a helmet and a bulletproof jacket as soon as his feet hit the ground.

He preached to hundreds of grimy, unshaven soldiers who were holding their rifles, ready if needed. On one hillside, he preached from a platform decorated with an enormous painting of Jesus watching over a Marine who had dropped his head on his arms as if to get a moment's rest during a battle.

The chance to meet with Korean Christians also impressed Billy deeply. At one place, wearing a fleece-lined parka and heavy boots to protect him from freezing cold winds, he spoke for four nights from an open-air platform to several thousand Koreans and American soldiers who sat on tiny straw mats or stood in the mud to hear him. He attended prayer meetings that began at five o'clock in the morning. He was shamed by Korean pastors, tears streaming down their cheeks as they gripped his hand to thank him for coming.

"I felt so humble as I stood with these men," he said. "I was not worthy to untie their shoes. These men had suffered persecution for Christ—their families had been killed because of their testimony for Christ—their homes were gone, they had no more worldly possessions—and here they were, coming to listen to me preach the Gospel and thanking me for it. They were preaching to me, but they did not know it."

Billy later said that he had "wept more" in Korea than he had in years. "These experiences changed my life. I felt as though I had gone in a boy and come out a man."

The next year, Billy wrote his first book, *Peace with God*. He wrote about many of the same things he talked about in his sermons. The book eventually sold more than two million copies and was translated into thirty-eight languages.

* * *

While Billy was building his career as an evangelist, Ruth worked hard to build a stable home for their growing family. In 1948, shortly after the birth of a second daughter, Anne, she borrowed $4,000 to buy a small house across the street from her parents in Montreat. A third daughter, named Ruth but known from birth as Bunny ("because she looked like a rabbit"), arrived in 1950. And in 1952, the Grahams had a son, William Franklin III.

With the help of her parents, Ruth gave the children great attention, but their father's long absences were hard for them. Once, Ruth brought Anne to a crusade and let her surprise her father while he was talking on the telephone. Billy stared at Anne with a blank look. He didn't recognize his own daughter. A few years later, when Billy returned home from a crusade, young Franklin, with a puzzled look, said, "Who he?"

The rest of the world, of course, knew who Billy Graham was. Curious tourists often drove past the house to have a look at the place where the famous evangelist lived. GiGi and Anne once stretched a rope across the road and demanded a dollar from everyone who stopped to look. Bunny had a subtler trick. Whenever a tour bus would stop by the gate, she would walk out with a little red purse on her arm and just stand there with a sad look

Saying good-bye to Ruth, with daughter Ruth by her side.

on her face. People almost always gave her money until Ruth saw her one day and put a stop to it.

When Billy was away, Ruth would tell the children that he had "gone somewhere to tell the people about Jesus." Their grandfather, Dr. Nelson Bell, a missionary surgeon, served well as a substitute father. But the children noticed Billy's absences. One day Ruth saw one of the girls sitting out on the lawn, staring at an airplane in the distance, and calling out, "Bye, Daddy! Bye, Daddy!" A plane meant Daddy was going somewhere. Ruth read Billy's letters aloud to the children, led them in prayer for him and his work every day, and on Sunday afternoons gathered together with them to listen to his voice on *The Hour of Decision* broadcast. Afterward, he usually called to talk with each one of them.

It was not easy, Ruth said. "How much we missed him only each one knows."

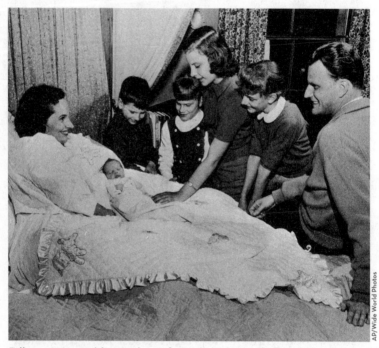

Billy saying good-bye to his wife Ruth and their five children on January 15, 1958, before departing on a crusade that would take him to eight Latin American countries. The children are, from left: Ned, four days old, Franklin, 5, Ruth, 7, Gigi, 12, and Anne, 9.

8

London and New York

As Billy's fame grew, the friends he had met in England while traveling with Youth for Christ invited him to come back to London for a full-scale crusade. But not everyone was happy about his trip. Some church leaders didn't like Billy's enthusiastic style. Others just didn't think they needed an American to preach to them about being a Christian. Even politicians and newspaper reporters criticized him, especially after his organization launched a publicity campaign that included almost thirty thousand posters with a picture of Billy and the simple instruction, "Hear Billy Graham." This was just too much.

Despite all the publicity and months of careful preparation by his team, which by now had grown much larger, Billy was worried that he was going to fail. The only place his sponsors were able to rent that was large enough to hold a typical crowd was Harringay Arena, a drab building used mostly for boxing matches. It was located next door to a dog track in a seedy section of London. Billy and his team feared that Christian people might not want to go there because of the neighborhood and its link with gambling, but they had no better choice.

On the evening of the opening service, as Billy and Ruth were being driven to the arena through a steady mixture of sleet and freezing rain, they held hands and stared glumly into the drizzly darkness.

When they arrived at the arena, no one was outside. Billy imagined he would be speaking to scattered clumps of supporters and a few mocking reporters. Just then, a team member came running toward them. He was excited. "The building is packed!" he said. "And thousands are on the other side trying to get in! They've come in the last twenty minutes from everywhere. Listen to them sing!"

The most remarkable religious revival in modern British history was under way. On only a few nights of the next three months did any of the twelve thousand seats of Harringay Arena sit empty. Each night, busloads of people traveled hundreds of miles to attend the service. Entire subway trains were packed with people singing, "To God be the glory, Great things he hath done."

To reach even more people, the team tried an experiment. They broadcast the service over the telephone to loudspeakers set up in a movie theater at the other end of London. It worked. They quickly tried it in other places, in churches and rented auditoriums.

After two months, the crusade was going out to 430 churches and rented halls in 175 different cities and towns in England, Ireland, Scotland, and Wales. Local church leaders at each location would lead the singing and prayers and take up an offering to pay for the cost of the telephone line and rental on their building. Then, when it was time for the sermon, the telephone link would be made. The people, while looking at a six-foot photo of Billy, would hear his voice over a loudspeaker.

Billy's team continued to use this basic technique in many places, improving it as technology changed. Eventually, Billy was able to preach to people all over the world by means of satellite television.

As the crusade in London went on, most people who had criticized and opposed Billy Graham recognized that he was sincere, and that many people were being blessed by his preaching. Billy's open friendliness, transparent sincerity, and disarming humanity transformed acid into warm milk.

One reporter admitted he had planned to be rude to Billy at an interview, but wrote, "He is not a man you can be rude to, for the simple reason that a voice inside you tells you that this is a man of integrity." Another wrote, "I never thought that friendliness had such a sharp, cutting edge. The bloke means everything he says."

Politicians and important members of British society invited Billy to speak to their organizations. Capacity crowds attended his appearances at Cambridge and Oxford universities. A rally on Good Friday at the famous Hyde Park attracted 30,000 people. And two services on the crusade's closing day drew at least 185,000 people to London's two largest stadiums—the largest crowds ever assembled for a religious event in British history.

Billy tried to meet the most famous and powerful man in England at the time—Prime Minister Winston Churchill. Billy had invited Churchill to the crusade and had asked to meet with him privately. The prime minister, who led Great Britain through World War II, turned him down. But the huge rallies had made Churchill curious about this American. On the last day, after the rallies were over, Churchill agreed to meet with Billy for five minutes. But no more.

Billy was nervous as he was ushered into the Cabinet Room at 10 Downing Street, the prime minister's residence. But so was Churchill, unsure what to say to an American evangelist. Billy, who was six-foot-three, was surprised to see that Churchill was rather short, but he still felt in awe of the world-famous leader.

Churchill twiddled an unlit cigar in his chubby fingers and looked at Billy. "I am an old man, without any hope for the world. What hope do you have for the world, young man?"

Billy took his little New Testament out of his pocket and said, "Mr. Prime Minister, I am filled with hope! Life is very exciting, even if there's a war, because I know what is going to happen in the future."

Churchill said little as Billy talked. He listened. Billy explained the significance of the life, death, and resurrection of Christ. He told Churchill he believed

Christ would come again to bring human history to a glorious conclusion.

The visit stretched from five minutes to forty. Churchill noted later that he had been impressed with the earnest young preacher.

And the young preacher had been impressed with Churchill. "I felt," Billy said, "like I had shaken hands with Mr. History."

The Harringay Crusade gave Billy Graham's career an enormous boost. By touching London, he touched the entire British Empire, whose long fingers reached around the globe. And by leaving his mark on this great world capital, Billy transformed himself into a world figure.

After Harringay, Billy preached in Sweden, Denmark, Holland, Germany, and France. In 1956, he visited India, preaching to huge crowds in several cities. In one place, Palamcottah, the crowds seemed out of control. Billy was frightened. Wherever they went, people filled the streets. They fought with each other just to get close to him. They pushed the car he was in so violently he feared it would overturn.

He also noticed another problem. He feared the people there were beginning to see him as a god. "Many of them fell down and practically worshiped me as I came by," he said. "Many of them tried to get in my shadow. I told them time after time that I am not a god, but a man."

The other great crusade of the 1950s took place in New York City in 1957. The crusade filled Madison

Square Garden with 18,000 people every night from May 15 to September 2. Nearly all of the newspapers gave the crusade great positive attention. The *New York Times* devoted two full pages to the first service and included a full copy of Billy's sermon. Another paper compared Billy to "an excellent salesman: he describes the goods in plain terms, lets you see them and decide on them. He avoids the old, ranting ways and the pulpit thumping. He is a skilled and wise and practiced sales-man of a commodity he truly believes should be in every home."

Clearly, Billy still remembered the valuable lessons he learned while selling Fuller brushes.

More than in any previous crusade, television played a major role in calling attention to Billy Graham. He appeared frequently for interviews on local stations. He also appeared on popular programs on the three major networks—CBS, ABC, and NBC. He even began broad-casting his Saturday evening services live over the ABC network. This gave Billy the chance to tell more people about Jesus. The popular broadcasts also gave Bev Shea the chance to introduce a new song to people all over America. That song, "How Great Thou Art," soon be-came one of the most popular and best-loved hymns in the world.

The many things Billy had to do besides preach ex-hausted him. He lost so much weight—thirty pounds by the end of the crusade—and was so tired that he started spending as much of the day as he could in bed so he'd have the strength to give the next sermon. One day, riding in an elevator, distracted and almost in a stupor, an attractive woman spoke to him. He barely noticed. Not until she got off the elevator did he realize who it was. He had failed to recognize his own wife!

Preaching to a large crowd in Times Square.

The Billy Graham crusades were breaking records. More than two million people attended the services in Madison Square Garden, with 55,000 making decisions for Christ. A special service in July drew more than 100,000 people to Yankee Stadium, breaking the previous attendance record by more than 12,000.

The long campaign finally ended on Labor Day evening, September 2. Billy spoke from a platform in Times Square. The crowd stretched up Broadway for blocks in a wide ribbon of people standing shoulder to shoulder.

"Let us tell the whole world tonight," Billy boomed, "that we Americans believe in God. Let us tonight make this a time of rededication—not only to God but to the principles and freedoms that our forefathers gave us.

Here at the Crossroads of America, let us tell the world that we are united and ready to march under the banner of Almighty God, taking as our slogan that which is stamped on our coins: 'In God We Trust.' "

9

They Are Precious in His Sight

As a son of the South, Billy Graham grew up believing that African Americans were different and inferior to white people. That's what he had learned. That's what he heard from the time he was young. But his parents were not extremely racist. Billy's father hired a black man to be foreman of the dairy farm. Billy worked beside him, learned from him, played with his children, and shared meals at his family's table.

The South was segregated, with even separate water fountains labeled for "colored." Billy did not seriously question racial segregation. It just was the way it was. Bob Jones College in Tennessee and Florida Bible Institute were for whites only. Wheaton College had originally been founded by people who wanted to abolish slavery. The student body included a few black students, and Billy became friends with some of them. In his anthropology studies, he learned that many of the things people believe are related to race are really shaped by such things as language, religion, and social values. Still, he didn't think it was his duty to oppose segregation. It was enough to treat the African Americans he knew with courtesy and fairness.

During the early years of his ministry, Billy followed local custom on segregation. In Los Angeles and Boston, blacks were welcomed and free to sit wherever they wished. In South Carolina, Georgia, and other southern states, they had to sit in a clearly labeled "colored section." This bothered Billy's conscience, because he knew the Bible teaches that all people are created equal under God.

Billy never wanted to cause a fuss. But he finally decided that he had to speak out against racism and segregation. At a national meeting of Southern Baptists in 1952, he shocked some people by saying that every Baptist college had a Christian duty to welcome qualified black students.

That summer, in Jackson, Mississippi, he preached that God's love knows no racial barriers. He called segregation one of Mississippi's greatest social problems. "There is no scriptural basis for segregation," he said. "The ground at the foot of the cross is level. It touches my heart when I see whites stand shoulder to shoulder with blacks at the cross."

Still, for a time, he continued to follow local custom.

But his knowledge that segregation was a sin pulled him toward doing the right thing.

In March 1953, he told the sponsors of his Chattanooga, Tennessee, crusade that he could no longer accept segregated seating. When the sponsors objected, Billy went to the crusade taber-

Billy relaxing at his mountainside home near Montreat, May 1, 1957.

nacle and personally removed the ropes that marked the section reserved for African Americans. A few months later in Detroit, African Americans served on various crusade committees, sang in the choir, and acted as ushers. Some black ministers sat on the same platform where Billy preached, a sign of his respect for them.

"The church must practice the Christianity it professes," Billy proclaimed. "The state, the sports world, and even the business field are way ahead of the church in getting together racially. Church people should be the first to step forward and practice what Christ taught— that there is no difference in the sight of God."

In 1952, Billy started writing a newspaper column called *My Answer.* When someone wrote to ask if the Bible teaches that any one race is superior, his answer was clear: "Definitely not. The Bible teaches that God hath made of one blood all the nations of the world." Christians should work to achieve racial justice, he said, and they should be doing it because the Holy Spirit has transformed their hearts and their minds. When true Christians look at other people, they see "no color, nor class, nor condition, but simply human beings with the same longings, needs and aspirations as our own."

This was a time when African Americans were beginning to protest. They marched and spoke out against not being able to send their children to the same schools as whites, not being able to eat in the same restaurants as whites, stay in the same motels as whites, attend the same movies and swim in the same swimming pools as whites, or use the same restrooms or even drink from the same water fountains as whites.

Billy was never comfortable with protest, even with nonviolent protest that made people angry. Still, he would always preach that all people are equal in the sight of God.

In 1954, the United States Supreme Court ruled, in a famous case known as *Brown v. Board of Education of Topeka, Kansas*, that segregated schools are unconstitutional and therefore illegal. In some parts of the country, especially in the South, this decision was extremely unpopular among whites. Many white people simply refused to obey the law for a long time. African Americans, however, thought it should have happened much earlier. They stepped up their demands to be treated fairly not only in schools, but in other ways as well.

Billy had long been fascinated by famous people, especially powerful politicians. In 1952, he encouraged General Dwight Eisenhower, who had led the United States and its allies to victory over Germany in World War II, to run for president. After General Eisenhower won the election and became president, he and Billy became good friends and often played golf together. The president sometimes helped Billy make contacts with important leaders during his foreign travels. When Billy returned from a trip, he would stop by the White House and give the president his impression of what was happening in other countries.

As racial tension grew in many parts of the country, President Eisenhower got in touch with Billy to talk about ways he and other preachers might help avoid serious trouble between blacks and whites. Billy agreed to use his influence. He began meeting with a wide range of black and white Southern religious leaders, urging them to find ways to adjust to integration peacefully.

Talking with U.S. President Dwight Eisenhower during a visit to the White House in Washington, D.C., May 10, 1957.

He also wrote an article for *Life*, one of the most

popular magazines in the country, urging parents not to pass on the sin of prejudice, but to teach their children to love people of other races. All Christians, he wrote, should "take a stand in your church for neighbor love. Take courage, speak up, and help the church move forward in bettering race relations."

During the summer of 1957, when Billy was preaching in New York City, he took an important public stand on racial matters. Boycotts and sit-ins led by the Reverend Martin Luther King Jr. and other black preachers were turning up the pressure in the South. Many people regarded Dr. King as a troublemaker.

Billy knew that some of the things Dr. King did made people angry, but he thought the young black preacher, by insisting on nonviolent measures even when people attacked him, was "setting an example of Christian love." In an interview, Billy said that those who say they love Jesus but hate people whose skin is a different color break the commandment to love their neighbor. And since they claim to love God, they are taking God's name in vain, breaking another commandment. He pointed out that since to hate someone is to wish that person would die, racists also break the commandment against murder.

These statements upset many of Billy's supporters, especially people who lived in the South. But he didn't stop with just words. First, he integrated his own organization by inviting Howard O. Jones, a young black pastor from Cleveland, to join his team. Jones organized rallies for black youth and a service in Harlem, a section of New York City where many African Americans lived. Billy spoke to a packed house of several thousand blacks. Before long blacks were making up about twenty percent of the nightly audience at Billy's Madison Square Garden crusades.

Billy with Martin Luther King Jr.

Billy then took another bold step by inviting Martin Luther King Jr. to visit with his team and to participate in a Crusade service. Dr. King accepted the invitation. That night, before a capacity crowd, Billy invited Dr. King to come to the platform and lead the congregation in prayer. In his introduction Billy said, "A great social revolution is going on in the United States today. Dr. King is one of its leaders, and we appreciate his taking time out of his busy schedule to come and share this service with us tonight."

That let both blacks and whites know that Billy Graham was willing to be identified with this social revolution and its most important leader. By appearing with him, Martin Luther King Jr. was telling blacks that Billy Graham was their friend.

At the end of that summer, as the New York Crusade was drawing to a close, the focus of the civil-rights crisis shifted to Little Rock, Arkansas. The federal government ordered the schools there to stop stalling and to allow African Americans to enroll.

Arkansas Governor Orval Faubus refused to obey. He ordered members of the Arkansas National Guard to stop any blacks who might try to enter Central High School. Nine black students had enrolled. President Eisenhower met with the governor, trying to get him to agree to allow the students to enter. He also issued a warning. He told Faubus that he intended to "uphold the federal Constitution by every legal means."

Governor Faubus withdrew the Guardsmen and even assigned state troopers to protect the nine black students who were trying to enroll. But a violent mob forced the students to give up and go back home. This turmoil continued for days.

President Eisenhower and Vice President Richard Nixon both talked with Billy about how to respond. When the president said he was thinking of sending federal troops to Little Rock, Billy said, "Mr. President, I think that is the only thing you can do. It is out of hand, and the time has come to stop it."

That afternoon, more than a thousand soldiers rolled into Little Rock to enforce the integration of Central High School.

Billy's support of racial integration angered many of the people who contributed to his ministry, but he did not back down. After racists bombed a newly integrated

AP/Wide World Photos

Enjoying an ice-cream soda with a group of teenagers after discussing the problem of juvenile crime at a New York City news conference, August 8, 1957.

high school in Clinton, Tennessee, he helped raise money to rebuild the school. He agreed to help lead an organization called Americans Against Bombs of Bigotry.

Later, in 1959, he went to Little Rock for two large public rallies. Though some wanted him to speak out more boldly against the opponents of integration than he did, a leading minister told him, "There has been universal agreement in all the churches and out across the city that your visit here was one of the finest things that ever happened in the history of Little Rock. So very many people have changed their attitude, so many people have washed their hearts of hatred and bitterness."

Later that same minister would write, "The influence of this good man was a real factor in the solution of our racial problems here in Little Rock."

10

Little Piney Cove

While Billy traveled around the world preparing people for an eternal home, Ruth stayed back in Montreat building an earthly one. In 1954, the Grahams bought a heavily wooded 150-acre piece of land on the side of a mountain. The next two years, with Billy in Europe and the Far East, Ruth bounced her red Jeep up and down back roads into remote areas, popping into gas stations and tiny grocery stores, asking if anybody knew of a log cabin she could buy. Some people thought it strange that the wife of their state's most famous citizen wanted to buy old houses. But she finally managed to find five cabins and several truckloads of old lumber, weathered bricks, and crooked fence rails.

Ruth had almost as much trouble finding carpenters who were willing to build the kind of house she wanted. Why would a woman whose husband had a good job want a house made of old logs? She should build a house with new lumber covered with asbestos siding or use clean bricks.

Ruth insisted that one carpenter hang old cabin doors on closets in the front hall. He quit. "Everything I've done up there I had to do wrong," he explained. "A man can't take no pride in this kind of work."

Other carpenters also thought it strange at first, but one finally admitted, "You know, this house kind of grows on you, and before you know it, you catch yourself a-liking it."

The house in Little Piney Cove, the name they gave their property, is easy to like. The view across the mountains, seen through great sweeping windows that fill the high-ceilinged living room, dining room, and kitchen, is priceless. The rooms themselves are large, warm, and rich with wood and books and mementos and the fragrance from four fireplaces. When asked how many rooms it has, Ruth would laugh and say that she had never counted them. "You have to decide what's a room and what's not a room. Ned [their youngest son, born in 1958] always slept in what was supposed to be the linen closet."

The Graham home was hard to find. Thoughtful neighbors learned not to give directions to tourists. But some made their way up the narrow, steep road to the house. They would knock and ask for directions, pretending to be lost. Some just wandered around in the front yard, hoping to get a glimpse of the famous evangelist or some member of his family. Ruth tried to

The family waves from their home, Little Piney Cove.

ignore them. If Billy happened to be home, she seldom told him they had visitors. If he spotted them, he often went outside to greet them and chat for a few minutes. Eventually, however, he agreed to install a fence with electronic gates to protect their privacy.

Ruth refused to expose her children to public gaze. They were not available to make comments to reporters. They were not trotted out on crusade platforms to tell adoring crowds what a wonderful man their father was.

And they had stern discipline at home. GiGi remembers spankings. Lots of spankings. "I got spanked nearly every day. Franklin too. Anne didn't seem to need it. She had those great big blue eyes that filled up with tears, and Mother's heart would melt. I usually started the trouble anyway. Mother was fair. She was particularly strict on moral issues, and respect for adults was a moral issue for her. But she had a great sense of humor, and we had a lot of fun. I have no memories of a screaming mother."

Ruth would be pleased at that memory, since she sometimes worried that she was becoming too harsh. She once wrote in her diary, "The children misbehave. I reprimand them sharply. The very tone of my voice irritates them. They answer back, probably in the same tone. I turn on them savagely. And I snap, 'Don't you speak to your mother like that. It isn't respectful.' Nothing about me commanded respect. It doesn't mean I am to tolerate sass or back talk. But I must be very careful not to inspire it either."

When Billy was home, which was less than half the time, much of Ruth's discipline went out the window. "Mother would have us in a routine," GiGi recalled. "She monitored our TV watching, made us do our homework, and put us to bed at a set time. Then, when Daddy was home, he'd say, 'Oh, let them stay up and watch this TV show with me,' or he'd give us extra spending money for candy and gum. Mother always handled it with grace. She never said, 'Well, here comes Bill. Everything I'm trying to do is going to be all messed up.' She just said, 'Whatever your Daddy says is fine with me.' We just slipped in and out of two different routines. As a mother, I look at it with wonder now, but it wasn't an issue. It was just two routines."

Billy's being home was also a different routine for Ruth. "They were always very affectionate," GiGi remembered. "Whenever he was at home, they were always hugging or holding hands, or he'd have her sitting in his lap. They adored one another, and it was very evident."

GiGi had a theory about her father's more relaxed approach. "Once, he disciplined me for something I did. I don't even re-member what it was about, but we had some disagreement in the kitchen. I ran up the stairs, and when I thought I was out of

Billy getting a kiss from his wife, Ruth, on arrival in New York on the ocean liner *Queen Elizabeth* on March 29, 1960, after a two-and-a-half-month tour of Africa and the Middle East.

range, I stomped my feet. Then I ran into my room and locked my door. He came up the stairs, two at a time, and he was angry. When I finally opened the door, he pulled me across the room, sat me on the bed, and gave me a real tongue-lashing. I said, 'Some dad you are! You go away and leave us all the time!' Immediately, his eyes filled with tears. It just broke my heart. That whole scene always stayed in my memory. I realized he was making a sacrifice too. But it seems like he didn't discipline us much after that."

Over time, Ruth reduced the number of her demands on the children to those she felt were essential. But she saw to it that all commands were obeyed, and she tried to be consistent. Even then, GiGi found it difficult to stay in line. According to Ruth, her eldest daughter "tried harder to be good than anyone—but couldn't."

Once, after a day in which she had been a real test, GiGi asked at bedtime, "Mommy, have I been good enough today to go to heaven?"

Ruth told her that we are saved because of God's grace, not because we are perfect. Later she admitted that she thought about telling her daughter that she needed to behave much better if she wanted to go to heaven. But she didn't.

Even when GiGi was misbehaving, she showed that she thought about religion. Ruth once caught her slapping her sister Anne on the cheek, insisting that Anne had a duty to turn the other cheek and let her slap it too. "Like Jesus said to do."

Another time, the three girls were arguing about who owned pictures they had cut from *TV Guide*. Anne and Bunny prayed and decided they should burn all the pictures rather than let them be a source of trouble. GiGi thought about it. She told her sisters Jesus wouldn't mind if they kept the best ones.

Not long after Ned was born, when GiGi was not quite thirteen, her parents sent her away to a boarding school in Florida. She admitted that she never adjusted well and "cried for four years," adding that "when Anne went away and cried for a few days, they let her come back home, but I had to stay all four years. I didn't like it, I was scared, and I missed my family, but the Lord led them, and I can't thank him enough now. I married young, and it was great preparation time for me. The Lord knew."

The girls' brother Franklin was turning out to be a real handful. He started experimenting with cigarettes when he was only three, picking up butts from carpenters working on his mother's dream home. A few years later, Ruth decided to cure him by offering him a pack and inviting him to smoke right in front of her. To her surprise, he quickly smoked the first cigarette down to a stub, then immediately lit up another one.

Other efforts to break his spirit were no more successful. Once, on the way to a drive-in restaurant in nearby Asheville, he kept pestering his sisters. His mother finally stopped the car, pulled him out, and locked him in the trunk. When they got to the restaurant, she opened the trunk. He popped out and said to a carhop who came to take their orders, "I'll have a cheeseburger without the meat."

Ned, who was six years younger than Franklin, was an easy target for teasing. Ruth once heard Franklin ask, "Ned, do you love me?"

Ned, always described as having a gentle spirit, answered, "Yes, my love you."

"Well, I don't love you," Franklin replied.

Ned thought about it a moment. "Well, my love you."

"Well, I don't love you!"

Ned knew where to go for help. "The Bible says—"

Franklin cut him off. "The Bible doesn't say I have to love you, does it?"

"Well," Ned said softly, "the Bible says some nice things."

That answer had an effect. Shortly afterward, while Ruth was tucking Franklin into bed, she noticed Ned standing at the doorway of Franklin's bedroom — Franklin had trained his brother not to enter without permission. The tiny figure shyly asked, "Can I come in and kiss you good night?"

This time Franklin accepted Ned's affection, and his little brother padded happily off to bed.

"You know," Franklin admitted to his mother, "he's a pretty good little boy."

To All Nations

After his great successes in the United States, Europe, and India, Billy wanted more than ever to obey Jesus' commandment to preach the Gospel to *all* nations. In 1959, he held crusades in New Zealand and Australia that attracted millions of people over several weeks. In Melbourne, Australia, the final service drew 143,000 people, breaking the attendance record that had been set there in the 1956 Olympics.

Television had come to Australia only two years earlier, and Billy Graham was its first national attraction. When Billy told people who wanted to make a decision for Christ to call a telephone number on their screen, so many calls came in that they tied up the entire telephone network for several hours. Observers said only Queen Elizabeth had ever received so much attention and admiration.

Early in 1960, Billy went to Africa. He spent two months preaching in nine countries. Crowds were small in some places, huge in others. In some countries, Muslims opposed his preaching and discouraged people from attending his services.

He also had to confront people who practiced ancient native religions, like voodoo. In Kenya, three men dressed as witch doctors walked up and stood directly in front of the platform where Billy was preaching. They stared straight at him as if they were putting a curse on him.

Instead of calling for police to take them away, Billy told them, "God loves you, and Jesus died on the cross for you."

They did not respond and their "curse" didn't work. Billy found out later that a newspaper photographer had hired the three men to dress up as witch doctors so he could get a colorful picture.

In Nigeria, a Baptist missionary invited Billy and his team to visit a leprosarium—a place where people with leprosy had to live to keep them from spreading that terrible, incurable skin disease to others. The missionary told Billy that Christians in the leprosarium knew who he was. They had built a "tabernacle" of tree limbs and straw. They hoped he might visit them and hold a brief service.

The village was filled with people whose toes and fingers and noses and ears had been eaten away by leprosy. Billy preached a passionate sermon, assuring the villagers that God loved them no matter what their physical condition was. He told them Christ had died to make it possible for them to have a new and perfect spiritual body in heaven. When he gave the invitation to make a commitment to Christ, dozens raised deformed and scarred hands to show their desire to accept the salvation he proclaimed.

As the team prepared to leave, a small woman with nothing more than stubs for hands came up to Billy and, with the missionary acting as interpreter, said, "Mr. Graham, before today we had never seen you. But since your London crusade in 1954, we Christians have been praying for you. Here in our leprosarium we have been keeping up with your ministry." Lifting an envelope toward him with two arms that had lost their hands, she said, "This is just a little gift for you and your team for your worldwide ministry."

Deeply moved, Billy held her arm stubs in his hands and said, "Thank you."

As she walked away, the missionary translated a note she had included: "Wherever you go from now on, we want you to know we have invested in some small way in your ministry. We send our love and prayers with you around the world." Inside the envelope was Nigerian money worth about $5.60 in American money.

Billy turned to look across the vast brushland. After a few moments, when he turned to his team members Grady and Cliff, tears were trickling down his face. "Boys," he said, "that's the secret of our ministry."

Wherever he went in Africa, Billy emphasized that Jesus was not a white man, that he belonged to all races.

Billy examining the huge pipe of a Joluo tribesman in Kisumu, Kenya, March 6, 1960, during his tour of Africa.

He would explain all the ties Jesus had with Africa: Jesus was born near Africa and his parents took him to Egypt for safety when he was an infant. Finally, as Jesus walked to his crucifixion an African helped carry his cross.

In Kenya and elsewhere, white and black Christians worked together to plan Billy's crusades and sat with each other during the services. In Northern and Southern Rhodesia, known today as Zambia and Zimbabwe, Billy insisted that blacks be admitted to the services. These were the first integrated public meetings ever conducted in either country.

Again and again, Billy told the mostly white crowds that the ground beneath the cross of Christ is level and that all who stand there are equals. "God doesn't look to see the color of your skin or how much money you have," he insisted. "An impartial God looks on the heart. He does not look on the outside."

Billy did not pretend that America had no racial problems. "Race barriers will ultimately have to end," he said. "I cannot presume to suggest a solution in the Rhodesias or in South Africa, because we have our own problem in the States. Before I can preach about color in Africa we must apply Christ in the United States."

He insisted that the only real solution to race problems would be a change of heart of the sort that comes only from true conversion to Christ. But he acknowledged that the laws and customs also had to change. "To keep the races in total separation is a policy that won't work and is immoral and un-Christian."

He added, "I would say the same of our past treatment of the Indians, as we look back on it."

Not everything about the Africa trip was serious or sad. Billy and Cliff Barrows whooped with delight as the little plane in which they were riding flew over great herds of elephants, zebras, antelopes, and buffalo in Kenya. The antics of a band of baboons made him laugh. Billy may have been reminded of the days when he played Tarzan in the woods behind the dairy barn back in Charlotte.

Billy went from Africa to Jordan, an Arab country, and to Israel, a Jewish nation. The two neighbors are located to the east of the Mediterranean Sea. Neither country had wanted him to visit. As always, Billy tried to be fair and to get along with both Arabs and Jews. "As a Christian," he said, "I'm both pro-Jew and pro-Arab."

This helped. King Hussein of Jordan welcomed him for a brief visit. A Muslim radio station recorded his sermon on John 3:16 — "For God so loved the world that he gave his only begotten son" — and played it several times while Billy was in Jordan.

The welcome was warmer in Israel, but Billy was asked not to mention Jesus when speaking to Jewish audiences. Billy said he planned to speak only to Christian audiences, and that he was not in Israel to try to convince Jews to become Christians. He pointed out that he felt a great debt to Jews. "Jesus Christ was a Jew, all the apostles were Jews, and the whole early church was Jewish." Although he was unable to rent a large hall for a public meeting while in Israel, Billy met and established lasting friendships with key Israeli leaders.

The African tour marked the end of a little more than a decade of preaching. At the beginning, Billy Graham was barely known outside evangelical Christian circles. He had now become one of the best known and most widely admired men in the world. A "clipping service" that collected articles about famous people from all the newspapers in the world reported that it was clipping more than five thousand articles about him each month, more even than about the president. Billy was clearly a major leader of evangelical Christianity and, in the eyes of many, of all Protestant Christianity. He had risen from preaching to drunks and troublemakers in saloons and jails to addressing tens of thousands in great stadiums. He had shared his faith quietly with kings and queens, presidents and prime ministers, famous businesspeople and celebrities of every sort. By doing that, he had helped American Christians feel that the United States was once again "one nation under God."

Traveling to different countries and meeting with Christians from many denominations helped Billy realize that it wasn't just Americans who were "under God." He wrote, "After a decade of intimate contact with Christians the world over I am now aware that the family of God contains people of various ethnic, cultural, class, and denominational differences. I have learned that there can even be minor disagreements of theology, methods, and motives, but that within the true church there is a mysterious unity that overrides all divisive factors. In groups that I formerly 'frowned upon' I have found men so dedicated to Christ and so in love with the truth that I have felt unworthy to be in their presence."

He summed up his message this way: "I have learned that although Christians do not always agree, they can disagree agreeably, and that what is most needed in the church today is for us to show an unbelieving world that we love one another."

12

The Power and the Glory

Billy had friends in the White House. For years in the 1950s and early 1960s, he met with President Dwight D. Eisenhower. During that time Billy also became friends with Vice President Richard Nixon. He hoped Nixon would become president and was disappointed when he lost the 1960 election to John F. Kennedy.

Billy and President Kennedy were courteous to each other but never developed a real friendship. When the president was tragically assassinated in Dallas in November 1963, Billy contacted Lyndon Johnson, who had been Kennedy's vice president and had become president. He told the new president he would be praying for him and was ready to help in any way he could during the difficult days that lay ahead. Within a week after the Johnsons moved in, President Johnson invited Billy to the White House. The visit, scheduled for fifteen minutes, stretched to five hours. The two farm boys who had each ridden their talent, ambition, and energy to the top of their professions found they had a great deal to offer each other.

President Johnson wanted to build what he called a "Great Society." He started programs to ease racial problems, help poor people, improve education, and reduce crime.

Billy approved. He said, "There is a social aspect of the Gospel that many people ignore. Jesus was interested in the hungry, the diseased, and the illiterate." He said Jesus spent a great deal of his time preaching about these problems. The church today, Billy said, should be deeply concerned about not only the poor, the illiterate, and the diseased, but also those oppressed by tyranny or prejudice.

Chatting with President Lyndon B. Johnson at the annnual prayer breakfast in Washington, D.C., February 5, 1964.

Billy believed Americans needed to be more concerned about poverty in other countries. And he had a warning: "Three-fifths of the world lives in squalor, misery, and hunger. Too long have the privileged few exploited and ignored the underprivileged millions of our world. Our selfishness is at long last catching up with us. Unless we begin to act, to share and to do something about this great army of starving humanity, God will judge us."

Hunger wasn't the only problem. Race relations in the United States had become tense and dangerous. Billy decided he had to do something. A few months after a black Baptist church was bombed in Birmingham, Alabama, Billy held a rally in that city's municipal stadium on the afternoon of Easter Sunday. About 35,000 people attended. About half were white. Half were black.

A week later, Billy spoke at the annual meeting of the National Association of Evangelicals. He said, "We should have been leading the way to racial justice, but we failed. Let's confess it, let's admit it, and let's do something about it."

Billy's words weren't enough for some. They criticized him for not taking part in protests and for not speaking out strongly enough in support of demonstrations led by the Reverend Martin Luther King Jr. (Less than five years after the church bombing in Birmingham, King was shot to death because of his strong leadership in the civil-rights movement.)

Even Billy was worried that he was being too cautious. He told a group of students, "It's true I haven't

AP/Wide World Photos

Chatting with former President Lyndon B. Johnson on the speaker's platform shortly before speaking at Texas Stadium in Irving, Sept. 18, 1971.

been to jail yet. I underscore the word *yet*. Maybe I haven't done all I could or should do."

A few days later he told reporters that, "I never felt that we should obtain our rights by any legal means, yet I confess that the demonstrations have served to arouse the conscience of the world."

President Johnson sent a warm letter to Billy telling him how much he admired him. The president invited him to come to the White House whenever he could. "Please know that this door is always open—and your room is always waiting. I hope you will come often."

The other great issue troubling the nation at this time was the war in Vietnam. Americans were fighting and dying alongside South Vietnamese soldiers who were trying to keep their country from being taken over by Communists from North Vietnam. Like the war in Iraq that began in 2003, that war was extremely unpopular with many people. It had dragged on year after year, costing many lives and billions of dollars. Billy wanted to support President Johnson's policies, but he grew uneasy with the long war.

Still, he knew the soldiers were doing the best they could and in 1966 and 1968, he visited the troops at Christmastime. On one of those trips, it was so cloudy and rainy that he had a hard time finding a pilot who would agree to fly him and his small team far into the jungle. They thought the bad weather made the trip too dangerous. Finally, someone agreed to fly them into some of the more remote areas. Several times, it looked like they had made a bad mistake.

"Once," Billy remembered, "we came straight toward a mountain in dense clouds. The pilot pulled the plane up as hard as he could and the tail scraped the trees. I looked over at Bev Shea and he was just sitting there. He's never afraid of anything. Nothing ever bothers him."

Public opposition to the Vietnam War was so great by 1968 that President Johnson decided not to run for reelection. Billy was not surprised. A year earlier, the president had told Billy that he didn't think he would live for another four years. He said he didn't want the country to go through losing another president, as it had when President Kennedy was killed.

"He thought a great deal about death," Billy said. "He talked to me about it several times. I had a number of quiet, private talks with him about his relationship with the Lord. Once, we were sitting in his convertible Lincoln, where he'd been chasing some of the deer right across the fields. We were stopped, looking out, and the sun was sinking. We had a very emotional time, because I just told him straight out that if he had any doubts about his relationship with God, that he better get it settled. I said, 'Mr. President, according to what you say, you don't think you have much longer to live. You'd better be sure you're right with God and have made your peace with him.'"

Johnson bowed his head over the steering wheel and said, "Billy, would you pray for me?"

Billy said, "Yes, sir," and he did.

Billy said that the president was very reflective after that. "We must have sat there for another hour, hardly talking at all, just looking at the sunset."

Later, during that same visit, President Johnson told Billy that he wanted him to preach his funeral. He also wanted to be buried right next to his father and mother in a small family grave plot.

The president then looked Billy in the eye. "Will I ever see my mother and father again?"

"Well, Mr. President," Billy said, "if you're a Christian and they were Christians, then someday you'll have a great home-going."

The president pulled out a handkerchief and brushed tears from his eyes. Then he decided that others needed to hear what he had just heard. He pointed out that there would be reporters and TV cameras from all around the world at his funeral. "Billy, I want you to look in those cameras and just tell 'em what Christianity is all about. Tell 'em how they can be sure they can go to heaven. I want you to preach the gospel." He paused. "But somewhere in there, you tell 'em a few things I did for this country."

Years later, as Billy recalled that meeting with President Johnson, he smiled with obvious affection for the powerful, complicated man who had also been his friend, saying simply, "He was quite a combination."

The next president to take over was another of Billy's old friends, Richard Nixon. As the Vietnam War became increasingly unpopular, so did President Nixon. The 1960s were a time when many people, especially young people, were angry—at the government, at the church, at business, at the police. They wore their hair long. They dressed in wildly colored clothes. They experimented with drugs. They had casual sex. They listened to loud rock music. And they did unpatriotic things such as burning the American flag or wearing a flag on the seat of their pants. Some refused to serve in the military. They marched. They protested. They were arrested and jailed. Young people have resisted authority and offended grown-ups throughout the ages, but this seemed to be much more serious than in other times.

Billy and President Richard Nixon wave to a crowd of 12,500 on Oct. 15, 1971, during ceremonies to honor Graham in Charlotte, North Carolina.

Plenty of conservative older people were ready to write these young people off as a worthless, even dangerous generation. But Billy wasn't among them. Large numbers of young people still came to Billy's crusades.

Billy decided he needed to understand the youth culture of the 1960s. He bought a stack of rock albums. After he and Ruth listened to them, he said he was surprised to find that a lot of rock music is "deeply religious." The lyrics ask, "What is the purpose of my life?" "Where did I come from?" and "Where am I going?"

He tried to mingle with hippies and protesters at several festivals and demonstrations without being noticed. He even put on fake whiskers to disguise his appearance.

Although he still regarded student radicals as a menace to society—he didn't approve of discourtesy and disorder—he came away with a mostly positive view of what he had seen and heard. He thought many of them showed "an unconscious longing for Christ" and were "asking the right questions." Even though he disapproved of some of their tactics, he insisted "they have a right to want to change the system."

Billy tried to help President Nixon. He invited the president to speak at a crusade. He helped organize an Honor America Day on July 4, 1970. The president returned the favor by traveling to North Carolina the next

Billy and Richard Nixon bow in prayer on the platform at the Knoxville crusade, 1970.

year to be the honored guest on Billy Graham Day in Charlotte. He also began holding regular church services in the White House. Billy thought this was a wonderful idea, but critics thought Nixon had done it mainly to appear to be more religious than he really was.

Those who supported the president were pleased by Billy's close ties to the Nixon White House. Those who opposed Nixon were offended. They charged that Nixon was using the evangelist to make himself look good. And Billy eventually came to realize, even though it pained him to admit it, that their charges were at least partly true.

When the president resigned from office in disgrace in 1974, Billy was crushed, partly because he felt sorry for his friend, partly because he finally realized that his judgment about Nixon had been wrong. He even thought his involvement in politics may have hurt his effectiveness as a minister of Christ.

Years later, Ruth called it "the hardest thing Bill has ever gone through personally."

Erasing Dividing Lines

For many years, Billy had refused invitations to go to South Africa, which had the strictest system of racial segregation, known as *apartheid* (keeping races "apart"), in the world. He finally agreed to go in 1973, but only on one condition. He insisted that there would be no racial segregation in his meetings.

In the city of Durban, 45,000 people from every racial and ethnic group in South Africa pressed into King's Park Stadium. It was the first large interracial gathering in that nation's history. Black and white people sat together with no sign of discomfort. One black Christian, eyes brimming with tears, said, "Even if Billy Graham doesn't stand up to preach, this has been enough of a testimony."

Of course, Billy did stand up to preach. As he had done in his earlier visit to Africa, he pointed out that

Jesus was neither white nor black. "He came from that part of the world that touches Africa and Asia and Europe, and he probably had brown skin. Christianity is not a white man's religion, and don't let anybody ever tell you that it's white or black. Christ belongs to all people! He belongs to the whole world! His gospel is for everyone, whoever you are."

The next day, the headline in Durban's major newspaper read, "Apartheid Doomed." (Apartheid as a law in South Africa ended in 1994.)

A few days later, in the city of Johannesburg, Billy addressed another crowd of blacks and whites—60,000 in all—the first interracial public meeting most of them had ever attended. The service was carried live to the nation by the state-run radio network (television did not come to South Africa until 1975). No foreigner had ever been granted that privilege before. The broadcast drew the third-largest audience ever registered by the network.

Two months after the South Africa meetings, Billy led a stunning crusade in South Korea. At the end of World War II, the Christian church in that country was small and unimportant. By 1970, Christianity was growing more rapidly there than in any other place in the world.

Today, at least a third of South Koreans are Christians. Eleven of the twelve largest Christian churches in the world are there, including the largest, which has more than 800,000 members. South Korea sends out more missionaries than any country other than the United States.

Billy's largest crusade ever: 1.1 million people in Seoul, South Korea.

Billy's crusade services were held on Yoido Plaza, a mile-long former airstrip that was usually reserved for military parades and events sponsored by the state. Billy's team feared that it was too large, that it would make even a good-sized crowd seem small.

But it was not too big. At least 500,000 people attended the first service. At the closing service on Sunday afternoon, attendance reached 1,120,000, the largest audience ever to hear a preacher in person anywhere in the

Billy Graham Evangelistic Association

world. Over sixteen weeks in New York in 1957, Billy had spoken to audiences adding up to more than two million people. Now, in only five days in South Korea, Billy spoke to more than three million people.

At the end of the last service, a helicopter lifted Billy from Yoido Plaza and skimmed over the mile-long sea of handkerchiefs and white programs waving at him from below. Billy looked down in wonder. "This is the work of God. There is no other explanation."

14

Behind the Iron Curtain

A major threat in the world that Billy often spoke against after World War II was Communism. From about the time Billy held the revival in the Canvas Cathedral, he preached against Communism, describing it as an evil force that enslaved people and wanted to destroy Christianity.

During World War II, the Soviet Union, a nation ruled by Communists, helped the United States, England, and other countries defeat the German armies led by Adolph Hitler. When the war ended, the Soviet Union—often just called Russia, since it was the largest and most important state in the Union—gained control of most of the countries next to it. These included Hungary, Poland, East Germany, Czechoslovakia, Bulgaria, and Romania.

The Soviet Union's Communist leaders claimed to believe in democracy, but in fact the state controlled nearly everything that went on. Most people had very little freedom. They were so cut off from the rest of the world that it was common to speak of them as living behind an "Iron Curtain."

The Communists in charge did not believe in God. They didn't forbid all religion, but they controlled it very tightly. They closed down thousands of churches and religious schools. Ministers had to be approved by the state and could not criticize the government. No missionaries were allowed to come from other countries. It was difficult to get a Bible.

To make things worse — much worse — the Soviet Union had a powerful military force equipped with nuclear weapons. The leaders were trying to spread Communism throughout the world.

The United States and the Soviet Union were the two big superpowers in the world. They both had rockets and nuclear bombs that could destroy the other country. And both were afraid that was exactly what the other country wanted to do.

From about the time Billy held the revival in the Canvas Cathedral in Los Angeles in 1949, he often preached against Communism, describing it as an evil force that enslaved people and wanted to destroy Christianity. Many Americans loved this part of his preaching. The Russians hated it. They regarded Billy as a real enemy of Communism. And he was. So, even though he wanted to preach the Gospel to people behind the Iron

Curtain, he didn't believe he had much chance of doing it. Then he met Dr. Alexander Haraszti (pronounced Ha-RAH-stee).

Dr. Haraszti was extremely smart and well educated, with degrees in medicine, literature, theology, and linguistics. He grew up a Baptist in Hungary, but came to the United States in 1956 and became a citizen. He had long admired Billy Graham. He had even translated Billy's book *Peace with God* into Hungarian. The two finally met in 1972 at a crusade in Cleveland, Ohio.

Haraszti had a mission. He wanted Billy to preach in Hungary. Getting Billy to agree was the easy part. The hard part was convincing authorities in Hungary to allow Billy to preach. For the next five years, Haraszti worked with religious and political authorities in Hungary to get approval for such an invitation. It cost him thousands of dollars. He made many long-distance telephone calls and traveled to Hungary several times.

The Hungarian authorities were skeptical. They saw Billy as "a burning anti-Communist" who wanted to stir up war. Haraszti disagreed. He showed them photographs and newspaper stories of Billy's visits to the troops in Korea and Vietnam. He pointed out that Billy had urged American soldiers not to behave badly toward people in the lands where they were fighting. He had prayed not only for the Americans and the nations they were defending but for North Korea and North Vietnam. He stressed that Billy no longer condemned Communism in the same harsh way he had in the 1950s. To prove that Billy had not embarrassed or caused difficulty in countries troubled by political tensions, he showed the authorities newspaper stories of Billy's visits to those countries.

Finally, in September 1977, with some encouragement and help from President Jimmy Carter, Billy spent a week in Hungary. He was a polite guest and an effective ambassador for the United States and for Christianity. He preached at several large churches. He met with Hungary's key Jewish leaders, who told him they actually had considerable religious freedom.

During a tour of a lightbulb factory, Billy accepted a souvenir lightbulb with the promise that it would shine in his home in North Carolina to remind him of his unforgettable visit to Hungary. He then said, "I have also brought a souvenir to you, my dear friends, something that shines much brighter than this lightbulb. I have brought to you the Light of the World, Jesus Christ."

Many of the workers began to weep. But these were tears of joy. Never before had any minister in Communist Hungary preached about Jesus Christ in a state-owned factory.

The high point of the visit came when Billy spoke at a large open-air meeting at a Baptist youth camp. There had been no advertising. People had spread the word, much of it by long-distance telephone. People came from all over Hungary and from at least six other countries. The crowd numbered about thirty thousand.

Billy did not criticize the Hungarian government. Instead, he noted that things were more open than he had expected. He said there was some religious freedom in Hungary. "I have not joined the Communist Party since coming to Hungary, nor have I been asked to," he said. "But I think the world is changing and on both sides we're beginning to understand each other more."

Billy's Hungary trip paved the way for other trips to countries behind the Iron Curtain. In 1978, he visited

Meeting with Pope John Paul II for the first time in 1981.

Poland, where he spoke to overflow crowds. He taught ministers and other religious workers in Poland how to do evangelism better. He returned to Hungary and Poland in 1981.

On his way back to the States, he stopped to visit with Pope John Paul II at the Vatican in Rome. That visit was the first time Billy had ever met a Roman Catholic pope.

In 1982, Billy was invited to Moscow. He had been invited to participate in a conference of religious leaders concerned about the possibility of nuclear war. The conference had been approved by the Communist Party and was designed to make the United States look bad. Many political leaders in America thought Billy should not take part in it. But he did. The first speakers attacked the United States, saying Americans were responsible for most of the problems in the world. They accused Americans of wanting to start a war.

Sitting on the platform in full view of everyone, Billy removed the headphones through which he was hearing the translation of the speeches. This made clear he would not listen to any more attacks on his country. Almost immediately, the attacks stopped.

Finally it was his turn. Billy stood up and looked out over the crowd. He said that the United States and Russia reminded him of two boys. The two were standing in a room knee-deep with gasoline. In their hands both boys held lighted matches, They were arguing over who had more matches. They also were arguing about how they might divide up the lighted matches equally. Yet they both of them knew that if either one dropped just one match, they would both be destroyed.

Billy called the building of more and more nuclear bombs "a mindless fever that threatens to consume much of our world and destroy the sacred gift of life." He said that even if neither country ever used the weapons produced, the hundreds of billions of dollars spent on weapons every year could have saved millions of lives by spending it instead on relieving starvation, poverty, and disease.

"If we do not see our moral and spiritual responsibility concerning this life-and-death matter," he said, "I

AP/Wide World Photos

Patriarch Pimen, leader of the Russian Orthodox church, listening as Billy speaks in Moscow's main cathedral, September 21, 1984.

firmly believe the living God will judge us for our blindness and lack of compassion."

The applause lasted for three minutes.

When Billy met with Communist leaders on these trips, he always stressed three things. First, he reminded them that even though Communists were in charge, they were outnumbered by people in their own countries who believed in God—not just Christians, but Jews and Muslims too. Second, Christians are honest people who work hard and are not a threat to the government. And third, Americans see religious freedom as very important. As long as people in the Iron Curtain countries were not able to practice their religion freely, it would be difficult for the United States and the Soviet Union to have a peaceful relationship.

In the years that followed, Billy visited other countries behind the Iron Curtain. Each time he spoke to large crowds. And each time he seemed to make some progress in persuading government leaders to allow their people to have more religious freedom.

One of the best events for Alexander Haraszti, who had worked so hard to get Billy to be able to preach in Hungary, came in 1989. An estimated 110,000 people jammed Hungary's largest stadium. Haraszti stood on the stage alongside the famed evangelist, translating his sermon into his native language. That service was the largest known religious gathering in that country's history.

Three years later, after the Iron Curtain had been torn apart, allowing gales of fresh air to drive out at least some of the stale air of oppression, Billy Graham fulfilled a decades-long dream. He preached to a packed crowd in the Olympic stadium in Moscow—the capital of Russia which had long represented the heart of Communism.

At one service, the famed Russian Army Chorus sang "The Battle Hymn of the Republic." The audience stood for the refrain: "Glory, Glory, Hallelujah, His truth is marching on."

15

Return to China

China was Ruth's goal. As she watched Billy travel the world, Ruth dreamed of returning someday to China, where she had been born and where her family had spent a quarter of a century. The people of China had never been far from her mind. She wanted to somehow help Billy spread the Gospel there.

In 1980, Ruth, along with her brother and two sisters, returned to the site of the mission compound in Tsingkiangpu, where they had lived in China.

But Ruth's main goal was to arrange an invitation for Billy to return with her. It took several years of careful planning, but she finally succeeded in 1988, with help and advice from many influential people.

To help them prepare for the trip, which finally happened in 1988, they got advice from former President Nixon, Vice President George H.W. Bush (who would become president in 1989), Chinese experts from the government and universities, the former Chinese ambassador to the United States, and an American man named Sidney Rittenberg. Mr. Rittenberg lived in China and was helping American companies that wanted to do business there. "He charges American businesses $7,000 a day for his help," Billy said, "but he didn't charge us a cent. He thought it would be a tremendous thing for relations between the U. S. and China for us to visit. He was the one who really started the ball rolling for us. He and his wife were visiting in California in 1979, and he saw one of our programs on television and said, 'Let's get that man to China.' And he started doing what Dr. Haraszti was doing in Eastern Europe."

The message the Grahams took to China was much the same as Billy had delivered in Eastern Europe. Before they left, Ruth described it this way: "First, we want to explain what Christians believe and help government leaders understand that Christians make their best citizens—the most reliable, the hardest working, the most honest. They don't get drunk and they don't run around or gamble away everything they make. They are good family people."

A second aim was to assure Chinese Christians that their efforts and successes were known and prayed about throughout the world. The Grahams wanted to help them feel they were a vital part of international Christianity.

And thirdly, Ruth said, "Bill will emphasize peace, peace with God. They talk about peace. They want peace. But they don't realize that they cut themselves off from the real source of peace."

The trip got off to a rousing start in Beijing, the capital of China. The Chinese ambassador hosted a banquet for the Grahams in the Great Hall of the People. The ambassador welcomed Ruth as a "daughter of China" and introduced her husband as "a man of peace."

The Grahams spent an hour talking privately with the head of the Chinese government, Premier Li Peng. They discussed the role of religion in China's future. Billy talked about his own faith in God. Premier Li said that he was an atheist but he admitted that freedom of religion in China was not as good as it could be. He agreed that China needed "moral power" and "spiritual forces" to help it become a more modern country.

The visit with the premier, which had not been announced beforehand, was reported on Chinese television and made the front pages of newspapers throughout the country, creating widespread public interest in the rest of the Grahams' time in China.

Billy preached, gave lectures, and spoke to groups of diplomats and business people. And, of course, the Grahams saw the things that all tourists want to see. On a visit to the Great Wall of China, a lively group of third graders entertained them with several patriotic songs. Billy thanked them and then asked one of his guides to teach the children to sing "Jesus Loves Me" in both Chinese and English.

When Billy joined in the singing, it was clear that he could not carry a tune. And he got the words mixed up

Singing with schoolchildren at the Great Wall of China, 1988.

in a funny way. If any of the children could understand his English, they were probably surprised to hear him sing about Jesus, "He is weak but we are strong."

An Australian couple recognized their fellow tourist, and the husband said to his wife, "What do you think he is doing here?"

His wife gave the right answer: "Probably what he does everywhere."

It's difficult, even dangerous, to be a Christian in China. When the Communists took over in 1966 in what was called the Cultural Revolution, they destroyed most copies of the Bible.

But rules against religious freedom were relaxing by the time Billy and Ruth visited. A Christian press was printing 600,000 copies of the Bible in that year alone and planned to print a million copies the next year. In each of the four other cities they visited, Billy spoke to large gatherings of Christians and met with key political and civic leaders. He encouraged them to remove all restrictions on religious belief and practice.

In Nanjing, Billy spoke to seminary students studying to become ministers. He urged them to preach the Gospel with authority—to preach it simply, boldly, and urgently, and to preach it again and again. They asked him questions. He answered their questions for a long time. Then they gave him a banner and asked him to remember to pray for them. Finally, one of the students said, "All of our students hope someday to be like you."

Billy spoke to large gatherings of Christians in each of the cities they visited. China had never received such a famous Christian leader before, and the Chinese media gave him lots of attention. His visits and speeches were covered on radio and television and in the newspapers. Ruth was interviewed by writers for magazines for Chinese women.

China has more than a billion people. No one believed that a large portion of them were about to convert to Christianity. But Sidney Rittenberg was pleased.

"Mr. Graham," he said, "is opening the big door for the advance of Christianity in China. In doing so, he will promote the opening of all the little doors."

16

What Manner of Man?

In almost every year after 1950, surveys found that Billy Graham was among the most admired men in the world. Billy was a true American hero in part because he was an example of some of the most basic values of American culture. He was easily the most successful evangelist in the world, but he reached that peak through hard and honest work, not because somebody gave it to him or because he was just lucky. He was always ready to use the latest technology—radio, then television, then satellites, then computers—to reach his goals, but he still insisted that the most valuable asset he had was a small circle of loyal friends, some of whom he had known since he was a boy. He knew kings and queens and presidents and prime ministers, but he always seemed surprised that anyone would think he was special.

Many people have tried to explain what made Billy tick, but he wasn't too interested in that question. "I am not a self-analyzer," he said. "I know some people who just sit and analyze themselves all the time. I just don't do that. I don't ask myself why I do this or that. I rarely think like that." Even though he may not have spent much time thinking about what kind of person he was, he thought a great deal about what kind of person he wanted to be. And the one word he would like people of future generations to use when they think about his life and his ministry is "integrity."

"That's what I've worked for all my life: integrity!" he said.

Of course, Billy was not perfect. He made mistakes. But he did try very hard to be the kind of person God wanted him to be.

Billy could easily have been extremely wealthy if he had been paid for giving speeches or had taken all the money his books earned, since nearly all of them were bestsellers. Each year he received thousands of invitations to speak. Many offered large fees. He turned down most of the invitations and took no money for those he accepted. The money most of his books earned went to his ministry and to various charities.

Billy's attitude toward money set the tone for his organization. Nearly all the members of his team lived in modest middle-class homes that gave no hint they were occupied by world travelers. The *Hour of Decision*, the most popular religious radio program in history, was produced in a little wooden building in Cliff

President Barack Obama meets with Billy Graham, 91, at his home in North Carolina on April 25, 2010.

Barrows' backyard. Cliff and another member of the team built it themselves. They also took care of the janitorial work.

Ruth was the same way. After watching her shiver on a crusade platform one evening, June Carter Cash (wife of singer Johnny Cash) gave Ruth a full-length mink coat with a hood. Ruth told June she could not appear in public wearing such an obviously expensive coat, especially not on a crusade platform. June said, "Wear it to the barn. Wear it in the car. Wear it out walking with Billy in the snow on the mountain. But stay warm!"

Ruth tried that for a while, using the coat for everyday wear, but she eventually got June's permission to donate it to a charity auction. Friends who knew what she had done bought the coat for twice its true value and gave it back to her. They told her that she was not to try to get rid of it again.

In a similar way, when several of Billy's wealthy friends offered to provide him with a private jet, with all expenses paid for five years, he turned it down. "Ruth and I couldn't sleep for thinking about it," he recalled. "We just felt our ministry couldn't have an airplane."

At home, even though they had a housekeeper, Ruth did most of the cooking. The food was delicious but not fancy—homemade soup, pounded steak or leftover ham, turnip greens and creamed corn, and marvelous biscuits she made from scratch. But Billy didn't require even that level of food preparation. "If I'm not here," she said, "his favorite meal is baked beans, Vienna sausages, and canned tomatoes. Can you think of anything worse? They're all the same color, for one thing."

He chuckled at his own simple preferences. "I share the beans with the dogs."

Billy continued to learn and to grow throughout his long life. When he was a young preacher, his answer to almost any problem a person might face was that "Christ is the answer." As he gained wider experience and thought about things more carefully, he admitted to his audiences that "coming to Christ is not going to solve all your problems." In fact, he said the change might "create some new problems. Because when you've been going one way and suddenly turn around and go the other way, against the tide of evil in the world, that's going to create some friction and difficulty."

One of the most difficult questions Billy and other Christians have to face is how to explain the great amount of suffering and evil in the world. Why do young people get cancer and die? Why do planes crash and kill innocent people? Why do hurricanes destroy entire towns? Why do countries go to war with each other? Why do wicked people blow up buildings or set off bombs in the middle of crowded shopping areas? Why do millions of people suffer from hunger and lack clean water while others have far more than they need?

Spending time in prayer.

As a young man, Billy blamed most of these problems on Satan. But as he matured and gained experience, he became uncomfortable with such an easy answer. He began to admit that suffering is often simply a fact that no one can fully explain. He wrote that Christians should remember that they are not protected from suffering. He admitted he had no answer when asked why some evangelists carried scars from being beaten and burned for Christ's sake, while he had been honored for preaching the same message they preached.

When asked how he would comfort parents whose child had been killed in an accident, he said, "I would put my arms around them and weep with them. I would try to tell them there is hope for those who put their trust in God."

One of his favorite ways to explain suffering was to say, "Picture a piece of embroidery placed between you and God, with the right side up toward God. Humans see the loose, frayed ends; but God sees the pattern."

Over the years, Billy's preaching changed. His sermons became shorter and simpler. He also used a much calmer and quieter style. Television was responsible for some of these changes. Because many of his crusade services were filmed to show on television, he couldn't walk around anymore, pacing back and forth. He had to stand behind the pulpit and keep his sermons short enough to fit into the time of the TV program.

His topics changed too. He stopped scaring audiences by talking about nuclear war and the fires of hell. He talked more about how being a Christian could help them deal with loneliness, emptiness, guilt, and the fear of death. In the early years, he was often described as an angry preacher. As an older man, he advised younger evangelists to "preach with compassion. People should sense that you love them, that you are interested in them."

Critics often described Billy's preaching as too simple. They wondered how he could be so successful. But people who watched him over the years believed that being simple was the secret of his success. They also thought that audiences could tell that Billy was completely sincere.

A respected English minister said of him, "There isn't an ounce of hypocrisy in the man. He is real. When I first heard him many years ago I wondered about the reason for his success. I finally decided that this was the first time most of these people had heard a transparently honest evangelist who was speaking from his heart and who meant and believed what he was saying. There is something captivating about that."

Another said, "I think people believe they are going to hear something from God when Mr. Graham gets up there, and I believe they do. They hear another voice through him—the voice of God."

Billy thought those descriptions apply to all true evangelists, not just himself. "An evangelist," he said, "is a person with a special gift and a special calling from the Holy Spirit to announce the good news of the Gospel. You're an announcer, a proclaimer, an ambassador. And it's a gift from God. You can't manufacture it. I study and read and prepare all the time, but my gift seems to be from the Lord."

As proof of that, Billy said that each time he gives an appeal "to get people to make a decision for Christ, something happens that I cannot explain. I have never given an invitation in my whole life when no one came."

According to Billy, giving the invitation made him very tired. "In the five or ten minutes that this appeal lasts, when I'm standing there, not saying a word, it's when most of my strength leaves me. I don't usually get tired quickly, but I get tired in the invitation. This is when I become exhausted. I don't know what it is, but something is going out at the moment."

Over the years, Billy's attitude toward various social issues shifted. He became more tolerant. He recognized differences among cultures. And he stressed forgiveness more than judgment. He also came to realize that changing social conditions can be as important as changing individual hearts.

Billy thought it was better for Christians not to drink alcohol because of the problems it can easily cause. But he also pointed out that Jesus drank wine and turned water into wine at a wedding feast. He admitted that he sometimes had a little wine himself before going to bed. He stressed the "little." "I only have to drink a little wine and my mind becomes foggy and I don't like it. After all, a clear mind is what I've been striving for all my life."

Billy also understood the power of sexual temptation. The temptations, he said, have always existed, but are especially strong in today's culture, where sex is so prominent in the movies, on television, and in books.

"It's very, very difficult," he admitted. "I think the only way young people can live clean today is if they have had a real experience with God."

He had some practical advice for young couples, perhaps remembering the evenings when he went out with girls in his father's car. He recommended that dating couples put a Bible on the car seat between them as a reminder. "Christ is the cure for even the most torrid of earthly temptations," he said. Once a couple makes a decision to resist temptation, "God provides a way of escape. The Holy Spirit is there to help."

Billy was always careful not to make people feel guilty about every sexual thought they might have. When speaking of lust, he said, "I'm not talking about looking at a beautiful girl and admiring her. That's natural. God gave us the sex instincts, and I don't think we should deny them. But He drew some circles around it and said, 'Thus far, and no further.' And if you do go further, you hurt yourself."

Billy's views about the role of women in the family and the church evolved considerably over time. In earlier years he spoke of the husband as "the master of the house" who "organizes it, holds it together, and controls it." He told wives "to remain in subjection" to their husbands.

By the mid–1970s, he had begun to change his position. He had listened to what women were seeking. He said his earlier views had been based on misunderstanding the Bible. With more study, he came to believe that "the Biblical position on women's rights is that the husband and wife are equal. Husbands and wives should 'submit to each other.'"

He disagreed with women who acted as if the role of wife and mother was not as important as working outside the home. But he also said, "There are things in today's feminist movement that I like because I think women have been discriminated against."

He also changed his mind on whether women should be ordained and become pastors. In 1975, he simply wasn't sure about that. Two years later he said, "I don't object to it like some do because so many of the leaders of the church were women. They prophesied. They taught. You go on the mission field today and many of our missionaries are women who are preachers and teachers."

As for women becoming full-time pastors leading a congregation, he said, "I think it's coming, and I think it will be accepted more and more. I know a lot of women who are far superior to men when it comes to ministering to others." Men might resist, he admitted, but such women "are ordained of God whether they had men to lay hands on them and give them a piece of paper or not. I think God called them."

In later years, Billy included women ministers in conferences his organization sponsored. He invited them to lead prayer and take other public roles in his crusades.

Billy's travels around the world made him keenly aware of the inequality between rich and poor people and between rich and poor countries. He said, "I had no real idea that millions of people throughout the world lived on the knife-edge of starvation and that the teachings of the Bible demanded that I have a response toward them. As I traveled around to India and Africa and Latin America and all those places for all these years and studied the Bible more, I changed."

Billy said the Bible, in hundreds of verses, makes it clear that God has a special concern for the poor of the world and tells us clearly what our responsibilities are. He wrote about hunger and infant mortality around the world. He called the differences between the rich and the poor one of the basic causes of social unrest in

AP/Wide World Photos

Spending time with the less fortunate in the village of Putthanpuram in southern India, February 1, 1956.

many parts of the world. Billy said it's important not to make people who can't find jobs feel like second-class citizens. "You can't have some people driving Cadillacs and other people driving oxcarts and expect peace in the community."

Billy never wanted to be the leader of any peace movement, yet he spoke often of the need for peace. From the beginning of his ministry, he preached against war. He called on Christians in every country "to rise above narrow national interests and to give all of humanity a spiritual vision of the way to peace."

He said President Dwight D. Eisenhower, who had been one of the greatest military generals in World War II and who knew that war is sometimes necessary, said, "Every gun that is made, every warship launched, every rocket fired signifies a theft from those who are hungry and are not fed, those who are cold and are not clothed."

Over the years, Billy became increasingly concerned about the threat to the world from nuclear weapons. He wanted the United States and the Soviet Union to get rid of all nuclear weapons. The two countries had long had enough nuclear bombs to destroy each other completely. In some ways, that made both of them safer, since they knew that if one started a war they would both be destroyed, just as he had pointed out when he compared them to two boys holding lighted matches in a room full of gasoline. But eventually, as a few other countries developed nuclear weapons, the danger grew. The careless act of one country could start a war that would involve all the other countries.

Billy wrote that working "to limit the growing threat of nuclear warfare seems perfectly in line with Christ's call to be peacemakers on the earth."

Looking back, Billy said he ought to have done more years ago to speak out against nuclear weapons. "In those first years of the nuclear age I did very little in this particular area. I preached the Gospel throughout the world, which was my primary calling, and I warned people against war in my sermons from the very beginning. But perhaps I should have done more. I wish now that I had taken a much stronger stand against the nuclear arms race at its beginning when there was a chance of stopping it."

He recognized that police and military forces would always be necessary in a world with sin, but urged world leaders to work toward eliminating all nuclear and bio-chemical weapons of mass destruction. He looked back at the meetings that leaders of the United States and the Soviet Union held, known as Strategic Arms Limitation Talks and referred to by their initials, SALT. The first of these talks lasted from 1969 until 1972, and were known as SALT I. A second group, held from 1977 to 1979, was known as SALT II. They made some progress, agreeing to get rid of some kinds of weapons and to limit the number of new ones they would make, but both countries still kept many weapons and could easily have started another terrible war.

Billy started calling for "SALT X." By that, he meant the countries with nuclear weapons should quit arguing over small changes—perhaps holding meetings called SALT III and SALT IV and so on—and just jump far ahead and agree to get rid of all nuclear weapons. He didn't really think that would happen, but he asked, "Does that mean I should cease praying, speaking, and working for that day when the people of the earth would unite to remove the ever-present threat of nuclear holocaust? No! I do not plan to be a leader in a peace movement or organization. I am an evangelist. But I am a man who is still in process."

That last statement was true of Billy until the day he died. Some people, as they grow older, decide they know all they need to know and don't need to consider new information or the views of people who differ from them. Billy was never like that. When he was a very old man, he said, "Much of my life has been a pilgrimage—constantly learning, changing, growing, and maturing. I have come to see in deeper ways some of the implications of my faith and message."

Those words and Billy's humble attitude help us to understand why so many people all around the world loved and admired Billy Graham.

17

The Last Days

As Billy and Ruth grew older, age and illness began to take a heavy toll. Still, Billy continued to hold crusades, going back to cities where he had enjoyed some of his earliest success. Most of these lasted only three to five nights instead of the eight days that had been customary even a few years earlier, and certainly not the weeks and months of nightly presentations of the landmark efforts in Los Angeles, London, and New York.

Although Billy was now an old man, his crusades did not appeal only to older people. Of course, many older people did attend these later gatherings, wanting to hear Billy Graham one last time. But again and again, in city after city, tens of thousands of young people flocked to hear him. Many came because their parents had told them they needed to hear this famous evangelist. But they also came because Billy had shown that he had a genuine interest in young people. When Billy traveled to foreign countries, he needed an interpreter to put his message into a language people could understand. He decided that, since most young people enjoy popular music, he would include more of it in the crusade services, letting it help communicate the gospel to a young audience.

For the next few years, Billy's crusades always included at least one Youth Night, featuring popular Christian entertainers such as Michael W. Smith, Kirk Franklin, and Steven Curtis Chapman. Each night they presented a full concert of high-energy music on a stage just like those at major rock concerts, with huge video screens on each side so that people sitting far away could still see the musicians clearly.

After the concert, Billy Graham would take to the podium. He would speak to the young people as a caring adult who wanted them to know that he understood their world and wanted to help them find purpose and meaning in their lives.

In city after city, Youth Night not only drew the largest crowd of the week's crusade, but set stadium records in almost every city. After more than fifty years of public ministry, the old evangelist was still "geared to the times but anchored to the Rock."

In 1996, Congress honored Billy and Ruth Graham by presenting them with the Congressional Gold Medal, the highest honor Congress can bestow on a citizen. The Speaker of the House called Billy "one of the great civic leaders of the 20th century." He praised Billy and Ruth for having "given up their lives as a model for serving humanity, and standing as role models for generations to come. By receiving this medal, you join about as exalted a group of citizens as we have in this country, and you frankly honor us by being here to receive it."

Frail and obviously moved by such praise, Billy said, "As Ruth and I receive this award, we know that some-day we will lay it at the feet of the One we seek to serve."

In 2000, Billy's son Franklin replaced his father as the official head of the Billy Graham Evangelistic Association. Franklin also heads an organization called Samaritan's Purse, which brings relief and support for people in need around the world, providing emergency supplies such as food, blankets, and temporary shelters after hurricanes, earthquakes, and other disasters. It also builds hospitals and schools in poor countries. Its Operation Christmas Child distributes millions of shoe boxes filled with toys to children around the world. Billy's other children, GiGi, Anne, Ruth, and Ned, also engaged in significant forms of Christian ministry.

The Graham children all acknowledged that their father had a difficult time growing old, not being as active as he always was. GiGi said, "In many ways, he has retired, but it's real, real hard for him to turn loose. It's just not the same anymore."

His daughter Ruth noted some of the same things. "One day I was at the house," she remembered, "and Daddy had been watching an old video of himself preaching on television. He said, 'As I watched myself,

I wondered what it felt like to have that power. I don't have that power and strength now.' "

But she added, "I think he underestimates himself. He underestimates the power of gentleness. There is a power in gentleness that is not in fire and brimstone."

Ruth noted that her parents had both grown more vulnerable as age and illness overtook them, but said they had always remained true to their natures. "Mother was always sweet. There's never a problem. It's all sunshine. She won't talk about herself. And that gets worse as she gets older. She'll never tell you how she feels.

"One of her nurses told me that she checked on her late one night and found her kneeling by her bed in prayer. She had every excuse not to kneel—her broken body, hurting and aching—but nothing would stop her from worshiping her Lord, and that's how she has always done it. On her knees. That's Mom."

Her father, Ruth said, handled sickness in a different way. "Daddy complains all the time. When he had shingles (a painful rash caused by the chicken pox virus), he was in so much pain and he would say, 'I'm dying,' and we'd all rush to his bedside. And then he'd get better. Finally, Mother said, 'Would you please just hush up and die like a Christian?' But it's so sweet to see him toddle in to kiss her good night and she raises her face to him, her eyes just sparkling to receive his kiss. Daddy is a clay pot that has allowed God to fill him with his grace."

Anne told a similar story. "Daddy just hates growing old, but in the midst of all his physical infirmities and limits, to see the sweetness of his character and the gen-

Billy and Ruth in their home in Montreat, North Carolina.

tleness in the same concern for others, it's incredible. It's such a testimony to a life that has been lived for Christ and focused on Christ, so that in the end you actually take on his characteristics. I look at my daddy and mother and I can see Christ in their faces. Sometimes when they are feeling the worst, are hurting the most, or things are not going right for whatever reason, you can see the countenance of Christ in them. And it gives me hope."

On September 14, 2001, three days after the terrorist attacks on the World Trade Center and the Pentagon, Billy Graham was once again called upon to be the "People's Pastor" at a National Day of Prayer in Washington. He was quite frail, and two men helped him to his place on the platform at the National Cathedral.

But when he spoke, his voice was strong, his manner sure. He said that when people asked him how God could allow such tragedy and suffering, "I have to confess that

I really do not know the answer totally, even to my own satisfaction. I have to accept, by faith, that God is sovereign, and he's a God of love and mercy and compassion in the midst of suffering."

After he finished, as he walked slowly back to his seat, the huge audience, silent throughout most of the service, signaled their respect and gratitude for the old evangelist with a sustained wave of warm applause, realizing that no one quite like a Billy Graham would ever pass their way again.

The dedication ceremony for the Billy Graham Library and Visitor Center on May 31, 2007, featured (from left) former presidents George H.W. Bush and William J. Clinton, Billy and Franklin Graham, and former president James Earl Carter.

In May 2007, the nation's major media traveled to Charlotte, North Carolina, for the formal dedication of the Billy Graham Library and Visitor Center. The mayor of Charlotte, the governor of North Carolina, and former Presidents Jimmy Carter, George H.W. Bush, and Bill Clinton praised Billy Graham for his contributions to the world and for the personal spiritual guidance and moral example he had provided them over decades.

The library is actually more like a museum. The house Billy grew up in was purchased and reassembled on the grounds. In the library realistic sets, photos, and artifacts gathered over a lifetime re-create key episodes and aspects of Billy's life. One room is devoted to Ruth's life, both as a young girl in China and Korea and as a devoted wife and mother in one of the world's most famous families.

Two weeks after the museum was dedicated, Ruth, surrounded by her five children and her husband of nearly sixty-four years, died at age eighty-seven. At her funeral in Montreat, Billy nodded toward her closed simple wooden casket, made by an inmate in a Louisiana prison, and said, "I wish you could look in that casket, because she's so beautiful. I sat there a long time last night just looking at her and praying, because I know that she'll have a great reception in heaven. Although I will miss her more than I can possibly say, I rejoice that someday soon we will be reunited in the presence of the Lord she loved and served so faithfully."

Ruth is buried on the grounds of the Billy Graham Library. Reflecting her plucky spirit, her gravestone reads, "End of construction. Thank you for your patience."

Billy realized that he would not live much longer. He said again and again that death held no terror for him, because he was confident it was just a passage to the glorious eternal life that he had invited millions of his fellow humans to share with him. He spoke of the matchless glories of being in the presence of God the Father, Son, and Holy Spirit, as well as the redeemed who had died through the centuries.

He talked of questions he wanted to ask God when they had a few minutes together, such as why there is suffering in the world.

He wondered about what people would say of him in the days and decades after his death, but only one compliment seemed truly important: "I want to hear one person say something nice about me and that's the Lord, when I face him. I want him to say to me, 'Well done, thou good and faithful servant.' I'm not sure I am going to, but that's what I'd like to hear."

Over the years of Billy Graham's long ministry, Evangelical Christianity became one of the largest and most vibrant segments of the world's religions. Many faithful and talented men and women contributed mightily to that remarkable development.

Still, from his crusades to the great international conferences, to the fostering of religious freedom in godless regimes, to the training of tens of thousands of individual evangelists, to the pioneering use of media, it was Billy Graham who, more than any other, shaped and inspired that movement. And he did so with a broad spirit that reached out to enlist an ever-widening circle of individuals and groups to join him in that effort. By inspiring Christians of every stripe and color and culture to work together in a common cause, Billy was a powerful force for Christian community. Individual lives and nations, the world, and the Church of Jesus Christ are richer because of his life's work. Truly, William Franklin Graham Jr. was, as Scripture says, "a workman who needeth not to be ashamed."